# CHRISTIAN OUTLAWS

James H. Henry

ISBN 979-8-89243-534-5 (paperback)
ISBN 979-8-89243-535-2 (digital)

Copyright © 2024 by James H. Henry

All rights reserved. No part of this publication may be reproduced, distributed, or transmitted in any form or by any means, including photocopying, recording, or other electronic or mechanical methods without the prior written permission of the publisher. For permission requests, solicit the publisher via the address below.

Christian Faith Publishing
832 Park Avenue
Meadville, PA 16335
www.christianfaithpublishing.com

Printed in the United States of America

# CHAPTER 1

## Teaching the Children

The campfire crackled, popped flames, flicked up and out, and created shadows. They danced on the cavern walls to the rhythm of the roaring fire. A group of young people, ranging in age from five to thirteen, sat in a circle around the fire. All their attention was on a grizzled old man who seemed to be beaten down and yet had the strength and vigor of a younger man. He has high cheekbones and a dimple on his chin. This old man with a heavy greying beard, that hangs down just past his chin, shoulder-length salt and pepper hair, crystal blue eyes, and dressed in blue jeans and a red checkered flannel shirt -smiled. Pain could be seen in his eyes for those who knew him, yet joy radiated from his being, the joy of being born again in Jesus Christ.

"Uncle Gene," said a small brown-haired young girl, "tell us the story of when we used to be able to worship Jesus in the open... before we lived in caves."

"Of course, Kaleigh, it is a story that we need to tell." The old man leaned forward and rubbed his hands near the fire. The cold and the years seemed to drain away from him as he began his tale.

"Well, you see I can remember a time when Christians were honored in our society. It was a time that almost everyone wanted to be a Christian, or at the very least, we were looked upon as someone that others aspired to be like."

The old man rubbed his chin and noticed that his beard had become white with age and scraggly. Wish I had some scissors and maybe a razor, he mused. He smiled again, but inside, his body shuddered from sadness at remembering a time when Christians were not hunted like animals.

He continued in a strong, rich baritone voice, "There were buildings, and some of them massive structures were set aside for the worship of Jesus Christ our Lord. We were able to go to these buildings called churches and openly worship, and we shared the good news all over the globe. Many came to know Christ during that golden age of Christianity, but, alas, that time has passed, and now we must worship our Lord in secret because of the laws that have been passed by evil people. However, children, what do we do for evil people those that don't believe in Jesus?"

All the children replied at once, "We pray for them and ask God to save them."

The old man smiled and gave them a thumbs up. "That is exactly right! Good job."

Another child about the age of ten raised his hand and asked, "Uncle Gene, why did the evil people pass laws like that? Don't they know that they could accept Jesus like we have?"

The man known as Uncle Gene lowered his head for a moment before he raised it and responded, "Some do know, and they decided to reject Jesus. Some of them can still be saved if they accept the salvation that Christ offers. They passed these laws because if they make us the villain then they must be the hero. If they are the hero, then we are the ones who are wrong, and they do not have to worry about atoning for their sins."

Gene looked around the room at the children he was teaching. *Father God, give them the wisdom they need to understand this next part.* His hands trembled as he used the stick to prod the fire, then spoke with a compassionate yet firm tone, "Before Jesus can forgive us for our sins, we must admit that we are sinners. That means that we must look at ourselves honestly. We must look into that mirror and admit that we are flawed, fallen, and sinful. We must admit that we are not perfect, we must admit that we are wrong. So to avoid that gaze into the mirror, people lie to themselves. They tell themselves that there is no God, or He does not care what they do. Satan's lies to humanity have always been God seeks to do you harm, God doesn't exist, or God doesn't want you to become as powerful as He is. Unfortunately, most people in our society today believe one version of these lies or another."

Uncle Gene took a deep breath, bowed his head, and rubbed his aging face. When he looked back up, he continued, "Do not believe the lies. You know God is real, you know that He loves you and seeks to redeem you, and you know that to think that we could ever approach God's power is to be foolish and arrogant. You know these things because you have God in your heart, and you can feel how much He loves you.

"However, people who do not know Christ have an empty hole in their hearts and their souls. They seek to fill it with whatever they can, whatever seems to make them happy, or whatever makes them feel in control. They have been made cowards because they believe in some government or man rather than the creator of the universe. They are frightened children that do not know who their parent is and do not know how to find Him."

The old man gazed into the fire. The charred and glowing red embers shifted, and with a shower of sparks roiling up from the fire, the old man continued, "The Bible, the living Word of God foretold of these days. In 2 Timothy 3: 3–5, it says, 'People will be lovers of themselves, lovers of money, boastful, prideful, abusive, disobedient to their parents, ungrateful, unholy, without love, unforgiving, slanderous, without self-control, brutal, not lovers of good, treacherous, rash, conceited, lovers of pleasure rather than lovers of God, having a form of godliness, but denying its power. Have nothing to do with them.'"

Uncle Gene sighed after he finished quoting the word of God. He had read these words many times, but he never thought he would see the time when it would come to fruition.

*Ah, mankind, you have no idea what you are doing. You sow the seeds of your own destruction*, he thought.

He looked up and saw the children looking at him expectedly as if waiting for the hammer of doom to drop onto them.

"Children," he said in a peaceful quiet voice, "do you believe in our Lord Jesus?"

"Yes," came the resounding answer.

"Then you have the Holy Spirit of God in you, and you will not be like those described in that verse. However, a word of warning, Satan is always trying to trick you, so stay in the word of God and spend time with God every day. Now back to the rest of the answer we are seeking today."

The children relaxed and riveted their attention on the old man again as he continued.

"The people who do not know God or have rejected God think that if they have enough money, power, or hurt other people bad enough, they have control over their lives, and no one can tell them what to do or hurt them first. What they saw was that Christians were at peace and had a joy that they could not understand. They sought to buy it, but they could not. They sought to force people to give them the secret of this joy. Christians shared with them the secret to their joy, but they could not accept the gift the Savior offered freely, so they became jealous of Christians, and they became angry at them. Most people will never blame themselves for their sins. They will blame others, and when this fails to make them feel better, they become even more angry at those people who have God's joy and peace. The enemy fuels this hatred because what is the first thing we learn about Satan?"

All the children around the fire spoke as one, "Satan is a liar. He hates your guts and has a terrible plan for your life." They all beamed with pride at reciting the mantra that Uncle Gene had taught them.

Uncle Gene looked out into the vastness of the cave lost in memory and said, "Bonus question, do you know who first taught that to me?"

The faces of the younger children strained in concentration while some of the older children simply smiled as they knew the answer but wanted the young ones to come up with the answer.

Finally, Kaleigh, the brown-haired girl who had asked for the story in the first place, slowly raised her hand.

Uncle Gene smiled and pointed at her. "Yes, Kaleigh, do you have the answer?"

She chewed at her bottom lip, unsure if the answer she had was correct, then blurted out all at once, "Dr. Bill Graff, a man you knew when you were our age."

"That is correct, Kaleigh." Uncle Gene leaned over and gave Kaleigh a kiss on her forehead. "You are so smart, young lady. You may just end up being smarter than me one day."

Gene laughed not at Kaleigh but at his self-deprecating humor. He did not consider himself to be smart or wise, he considered the Holy Spirit gave him inspiration and insight, and he was always happy to share those things with people.

"Now," Uncle Gene continued, "when you hate someone and you seek the things of this world such as money and power, the easiest way to obtain those things is to make people afraid. When you make people afraid, they will give you whatever you want just so they can feel safe."

Again, a shudder of sadness swept through the old man, but when he spoke again, it was with the same joyful smile that he always had on his lips.

"So what happened was those that were in charge kept telling people to be afraid of this or that thing so that the people would give them money or power or both so the scary things would go away. Well, Christians are not supposed to live in fear because we have Christ on our side, and He always works things out for our good. So when Christians started to tell people that the fear was a lie, the people in charge made Christians out to be the bad guys. They told people that we hated them, that we were the source of all their woes, and that we sought to destroy them."

A young man with blue eyes and brown hair spoke up and asked, "Why would people believe those lies, Uncle Gene? Why would they want to?"

"Satan is the father of lies. The Bible tells us so in John 8:44, 'When he lies, he speaks his native tongue, for he is a liar and the father of lies.'"

"When you do not have Christ in your heart, you are more apt to believe those lies. Plus, people had lost the ability to think for themselves, and they wanted someone to take care of them. They no longer wanted to be held accountable for their actions, but they wanted to always blame someone else for the wrong that they were doing. So along comes those in power, and they say, 'There, there are the people responsible for all the bad in the world,' and most people believed them. So they passed laws that made Christianity illegal. That is when the hunts and the bounties began. It is why we must live as we do. Do not be afraid children for you serve the God of all creation; however, be on guard."

A sandy-haired boy of three stood up and shouted while he stamped his foot, "Stupid laws!"

Uncle Gene grinned, walked over, picked up the young boy, and hugged him. The boy hugged him back and grinned back at the old man. Uncle Gene sat the boy down and then knelt, so he was eye to eye with him.

"Yes, Troy, they are stupid laws. They are laws based on lies and serve only those that passed them, not the people."

"So what are we supposed to do, Uncle Gene?" asked Kaleigh.

Gene looked at Kaleigh with a smile, but his eyes were steely as he spoke. "We are to do as our Lord Jesus has commanded us. We are to continue to spread His message of salvation and to patiently wait for His return. There are still many who will come to know Jesus, and it is up to us who already know Him to spread the good news."

"How are we supposed to do that when we cannot speak openly, meet openly, or even go out in public for long?" asked a voice from the shadows.

As he spoke, he stepped out and a man of about twenty-four years with red hair, green eyes, and freckles, dressed in tan heavy work pants, tan work boots, a blue tee shirt with a blue denim jacket, stepped into the blaze of fire light. He had a slender build, but the build belied the wiry muscles. He was stronger than he looked.

Uncle Gene smiled and gestured for the rest of the children around the fire to stand.

"Children, who do we serve?"

"Jesus Christ, Lord of lords and King of kings," came the enthusiastic shout.

Uncle Gene nodded his head in approval and the affirmative.

"Children, can any weapon forged against us prosper?" he asked.

"No!" came the shout louder this time.

"That is right," Uncle Gene said. "Where do we get these promises from? How do we know this is true?"

Several of the children answered at once, and some lagged their fellows. "From Jesus, He told us in the Bible."

Uncle Gene sat and bid the children to do the same with a wave of his hand toward the ground. "You all have been doing very well with your Bible studies. I am so proud of you."

Once all the children had seated themselves, Uncle Gene continued, "How do we witness to others even now? We rely on God to bring those that He has chosen to us, and we seek the lost sheep that He has decreed will be saved. We are always on the watch for those who seek our Lord and Savior Jesus. Remember what Jesus taught His disciples when He sent them out to witness.

"'I am sending out like sheep among wolves. Therefore, be as shrewd as snakes and innocent as doves.' Jesus told His disciples this in Matthew 10:16. It was right before He sent them out to witness on their own for the first time."

Uncle Gene poked a stick into the fire again and gazed into it for a time. The children sat still, but some were getting antsy and began to whisper among themselves until Uncle Gene spoke again, "We do not wait in vain. Jesus will return one day, and He has told us by His Word, the Bible, that every knee shall bend, and every head will bow, and all will acknowledge Him as King of kings and Lord of lords.'"

Uncle Gene looked at each face around the fire. He always wanted to commit each face to memory as they were right now, full of hope, full of God's holy spirit. It brought him great joy.

"Now enough of these stories, it is time for your schoolwork to start. Off with you now."

There was a general descension among the children. Some stated, "Schoolwork is boring. We want more stories."

To this, there were shouts of yes and please.

One child stated, "But I learn more listening to you, Uncle Gene."

Again, shouts of affirmation at this statement.

Uncle Gene stood and, in a gentle voice, said, "Go now, do as you are asked, and be joyful in the doing of it."

With that, each child started filing out of the cave. The man who had come in and asked the questions about how to witness came over clasped Uncle Gene on his shoulder and said, "You are amazing as always, Uncle Gene. I wished time allowed for me to come and listen to you as I did when I was younger."

Uncle Gene patted the younger man on the cheek and said, "You are always welcome, Johnathan, and it is not *I* who is amazing, it is God's holy spirit that speaks through me. Give God the honor and praise always. Besides, God has equipped you well, and you must be about His work."

Jonathan knelt by the fire and began preparations for tea. He looked up at his mentor and brother in Christ and saw that Uncle Gene's face looked as if he was having a conversation, but no words escaped his lips.

Uncle Gene asked silently in his mind, *When, Lord?*

*Soon*, came the reply.

# CHAPTER 2

## The Start of a Perfect Day

The caves that God had led the believers to were perfect. They were far enough into the forest that they would not be stumbled upon, yet close enough to the city that the believers could go into the city when they needed to. Gene and Jonathan were to make such a trip today.

As they walked through the cave, Gene heard laughter and conversations and smelled the bread and stew for the evening meal being prepared. He saw a community of believers that cared for one another. *Thank You, Lord, for blessings such as these people and this place.*

As Gene stood at the entrance to the cave, he mused on how perfect a hiding place this was. He thought aloud as he said, "What is it that David said about God in Psalm 31:20? Ah, yes, 'In the shelter of your presence, you hide them from the intrigues of men; in your dwelling, you keep them safe from accusing tongues.'"

Trees came right up to the entrance to the cave; however, when you stood at a certain spot, you could see the expanse of countryside below. You could see the river where they drew water from, you could see the small city on the other side of the river, and you could see the sun rising over the mountains to the east and just starting to bathe the valley in wonderous yellows, pinks, oranges, and reds.

Gene turned his eyes toward the sky and, in a clear voice, said, "Thank You, Jesus, for Your provision, protection, and the glorious painting You paint each morning."

Uncle Gene's musings were cut short as Jonathan placed his hand on Uncle Gene's shoulder. "Are you ready, Uncle?"

Uncle Gene never surprised by anyone's approach simply stated, "Yes, nephew, let us go see what God has for us this day."

Jonathan patted the old man on the shoulder and said, "You know you don't have to come with me. I can get one of the others to help. It is dangerous for you if you are recognized, Uncle."

Uncle Gene scoffed at this, "Nonsense, I need to work these bones from time to time. Besides, I think God wants me to get out of that cave for a while. It would not do for me to go stir-crazy. Besides, God protects us. If God wants, He can take my life right now, and I will be happy to see Him in glory. Do not live your life in fear, Jonathan.

"God tells us in Isaiah 43:1, 'Fear not, for I have redeemed you; I have summoned you by name, you are mine.'"

"Yes, Uncle, I know this, but I still worry about you."

Uncle Gene patted Jonathan's face and smiled. "That is because I am a joy to have around, and you would miss me."

Jonathan laughed, and then Gene joined in.

"Yes, Uncle, you are a joy indeed," Jonathan said as he wiped tears of laughter from his eyes.

As they walked, Jonathan asked, "Uncle Gene, how do we know that what the government and what the majority of people are doing is evil?"

"Good question, my boy." Gene opened his satchel that he had slung across his shoulder, dug into it, and produced two apples. One he handed to his walking companion, and the other he took a big bite off and relished the flavor and the juices running down his whiskers and chin.

Jonathan took the apple, took a small bite, and waited. He knew from experience that when you asked Uncle Gene a question such as this, that old man would take his time to answer. Jonathan often wondered if he did it so they understood that they may not like the answer, so Uncle Gene gave them time to withdraw the question.

Gene wiped his chin with the back of his hand, and when he had finished, he spoke, "The Bible, the Holy Word of God tells us times such as these will happen. It describes to us what evil is and how it manifests itself in our world, but, my boy, you know these scriptures and I will leave it to you to explore them and let God reveal to you what He wants to tell you about such things. Let's, for now, do a simple comparison. First and foremost, God teaches us to love Him and love our fellow man. Would you agree with that statement?"

Jonathan took another bite of the apple and responded, "Yes, sir, I would."

"The world teaches us to hate everyone. Hate someone because of the color of their skin, hate someone because they don't agree with you, hate someone because of the way they wear their hair, hate someone because they do not obey the government, hate someone because they follow Christ. The list of hates goes on and on.

"Satan cultivates and manipulates fear, hopelessness, and suspicion in the hearts of men. God gives love, faith, hope, mercy, grace, joy, and peace in the hearts of men. Whenever you are trying to discern someone's motives or your actions, ask yourself, 'Do these things generate those things of God or Satan?'"

Gene thought for a moment, took a last bite of his apple, and threw the core into the forest.

"Thank You, Father, that was delicious," he said and raised his hands to heaven.

Jonathan smiled and was always amazed that no matter the circumstances, Uncle Gene always gave thanks to God. Jonathan aspired to be more like that. He aspired to give thanks for everything, but there were so many things in this world right now that he just could not give thanks for. The situation for the group of Christians was getting worse by the day. More and more people believed that Christians were responsible for the ills of this world. His people were becoming more and more ostracized from society. It made things difficult, it made getting food and clothes difficult, it made staying free difficult, and it made staying in God's peace difficult.

All Christians across the globe were being hunted. Huge bounties were being placed on their heads, and if you could bring in one of their leaders, you could live like a king from the money you would make. Most were being imprisoned, but some were being killed.

Gene looked at his traveling companion and saw the worried look on his face. He knew what the young man was thinking about, but he would come back to that.

"Let's look at another comparison."

Jonathan's attention snapped back to Uncle Gene, and he once again was listening intently as they walked.

"God tells us to obey Him. Man tells us to obey man. God tells us there is sin, that we live in a fallen world, and Jesus is the only way to redemption with the Father. The world tries to convince us that there is no sin and that whatever we do is okay. That we are just animals, so we are justified in following whatever thing pops into our heads to do. Basically, it boils down to this—these things the world tells us are okay, but all have one thing in common, they are anti-God. Anything that is anti-God, comes from Satan, it is a lie and is evil."

Jonathan smiled. "You have a way of putting things in the simplest terms, Uncle Gene."

Uncle Gene patted Jonathan's cheek. "Ah, my boy, it is not I, it is God. God is not complicated. His word all comes down to, He loves us, wants a relationship with us, and wants to save us so we can live with Him in eternity. We can spend a lifetime coming to that understanding. I still am trying to understand, but each day I pray that I will have a closer relationship with God, and He will provide all I need to become closer to Him."

The trees began to thin a bit as they walked along the trail. Another couple of twists and turns and they would see a paved road that would take them into the city. It was autumn now. The evergreen's needles drooped some but remained green, the other trees in the forest exploded in color from brown to yellow, and it was beautiful.

Gene's favorite times of year were autumn and spring. The air was cooler, and there was a cleanness about it. "Thank You, Jesus."

Jonathan glanced over at Uncle Gene and then asked, "Uncle Gene, how do you give thanks for everything? I mean I understand giving thanks for the weather, the trees, the beautiful day, but how do you give thanks for everything? I mean do you realize the situation we find ourselves in? I sometimes wonder if God has just set all of this in motion and sits back and waits for the end to come."

Uncle Gene stopped, raised a weathered callused hand, and smacked Jonathan on the back of his head. It was just enough of a smack to focus the young man's attention.

"Hey, ow," Jonathan complained, as he stopped walking as well. "Why did you do that?"

"I did that so you would stop acting like a nonbeliever."

"What did I do? All I said was, 'How do you give thanks for everything?'"

Uncle Gene waved a single index finger through the air in a no, no, no signal. "That is not all you said. You said that God does not care about us, and that, my boy, I will not tolerate among my brothers and sisters in Christ."

"I did not..." Jonathan's words drifted off in midsentence, as he realized what he had said about God setting things in motion and then just watching. "Uncle Gene, I am so sorry."

Uncle Gene patted him on the cheek. "Ah, Jonathan, do not apologize to me. Apologize to God and ask His forgiveness. He will forgive you."

Jonathan bowed his head and prayed. "Lord Jesus, I am sorry for my doubt, and I am sorry for thinking you do not care. Please forgive me in Jesus's name. Amen."

Uncle Gene looked at the young man and said, "Better, my boy, better."

They began to walk again. "Now as to your question. How do I give thanks for everything? Believe me when I tell you there was a time that I did not. There was a time when I complained a lot, and some may say I even whined about my circumstances."

Jonathan grunted in laughter. "You whine? I find that hard to believe."

Gene gave Jonathan a playful punch and continued. "Do you want to hear this or not?"

Jonathan gave a mock look of contrition and said, "Yes, sir."

With a grunt of satisfaction, Uncle Gene continued, "The Bible tells us in Romans 8:28 that 'we know that in all things, God works for the good of those who love Him, who have been called according to His purpose.' For me, it is not just that Bible verse, it is that God has proven to me over the years that no matter what my circumstances are or how painful they are now, He works all things to my good, so I trust in the Lord. I know that the circumstances do not look good for those of the faith, but Jesus told us that we would be hated because of Him. He also told us that in the last days, men would turn their backs on God and persecute the righteous. Even as the bounties increase, even as our brothers and sisters are thrown into prison, yes, even as our brothers and sisters are murdered. We must all continue to trust in our Lord and Savior Christ Jesus."

Jonathan pondered Uncle Gene's words for a moment, then said, "Uncle Gene, it is hard to give thanks for hardship and persecution."

Uncle Gene's look was one of sympathy, his eyes dropped in pain and contemplation. "Believe me, I know, boy, but perhaps this will help. We know Jesus is going to return, correct?"

Jonathan nodded his head and said, "Yes, sir."

"Would it help you give thanks for all things if you realized that each persecution, each person brought to Jesus, each person that dies for the faith, brings us a step closer to our Lord returning to this earth?"

Gene's eyebrows raised in a questioning fashion. He was pleased when he saw his young brother in Christ slowly nod and say, "Well, when you put it that way, how can I not be thankful?"

Uncle Gene put his arm around Jonathan's shoulder and said, "That's what I am talking about, enthusiasm for the Lord's plan and willingness to do good no matter what. Now let's go get some grub for the troops. Even Christians have to eat."

They turned left onto the paved road and sang an old hymn as they walked toward the city.

# CHAPTER 3

## A Trip to the Market

The city used to be a vibrant place, full of lights, sounds, and the bustling of people. Five years ago, there had been close to a million people in this city, now only half of that remains. The city was split into two different areas.

Those who had enough money to pay for private security lived in nice houses with what could only be described as compound defenses in place. Some had electrified fences, some had walls with Constantine wire across the top, but all of them had cameras mounted on every approach.

The lie of the oppressors was fresh on their lips each morning, help the little guy, help the poor. All the while not lifting a finger or spending a dime of their wealth to help anyone. The age-old battle of class wars had finally come down to this, those who had gotten more could protect themselves by purchasing freedom and safety, or so they thought.

If you could not afford the luxury of armed guards and electrified fences, then you lived in fear of someone taking what little you possessed. Those that did not have the money, lived in houses, apartments, and even the streets. They had no security systems except for the weapons they carried on their person. Guns had been outlawed, but that did not keep people from carrying them or other things to keep the gangs and less reputable citizens from victimizing them.

The streets had once been kept relatively clean by the sanitation department. Now there was no such entity in the city. Garbage and worse were piled up on the sidewalks and flowed over into the streets. The smell was enough to make you hurl up your lunch, unless your nose didn't work, or you covered your face with cloth. Uncle Gene and Jonathan had to be careful where they walked and took short breaths to limit the impact of the smell.

The streets that had once been kept relatively safe by a police force were now patrolled by gangs and militia. The lie of criminals had more rights than the victims and more rights than the police who tried to arrest them had permeated a lawless and lost society. Anarchy and chaos now ruled the city. The fear and hate preached by the politicians and by the media that served them had done its job. It had turned a once-free country into a government-run hell. The politicians had what they wanted, power, the media had what they wanted, control over most people's minds. Those in power had no morals, no ethics anymore. Those in the media only lived to inflate their own egos, their drug was fame, and they would do anything and hurt anyone to make sure they got their next fix.

Between the rich sections and the poor sections, a makeshift market had been established. It was here that Uncle Gene and Jonathan were headed. They planned to sell what they could through money or bartering so they could get some foodstuff that they could not grow, they also needed medicines and bandages badly.

The place was set up like a farm market, there were tables and stalls that stretched for a mile. Wide alleys ran in between the tables and stalls and made a natural shopping aisle. Baskets of fruits and vegetables sat on inclined tables. Fresh meat hung from hooks and people were shopping up and down the entire length of the market.

From Gene's perspective, there was one thing that was looming in its absence. There was not too little conversation between the patrons. There was very little conversation between the vendors and the patrons.

Gene closed his eyes and remembered. Colorful banners hung from the stalls, people calling out to each other, stopping to talk to one another, and asking about their families, asking about why they were at the market, and if they could help them in any way. The smells of cooking bread and popcorn were always present. You could hear the young in the crowd asking for caramel popcorn.

The children were what Gene remembered most; they saw this trip as an adventure and always tried to escape the watchful eye of their parents. When they escaped the running and the chasing began, it was not the parents chasing the kids, it was kids chasing kids. Epic games of tag and closely contested races were a constant joy and menace for every shopkeeper. Gene could hear them shouting at the kids, "Hey, watch it!" "Where are your parents?" "I'm going to skin you kids alive if I catch you." However, Gene also remembered the smiles that crept onto the faces of those vendors once the kids ran past.

It was an atmosphere of joy and sharing, and it was in the past.

Now the silence fell over the place like a deep dank fog. People no longer lifted their heads and said hello to someone. They kept their heads down to avoid any eye contact with anyone. Hope and trust had been replaced with fear and loathing. The only hope they shared now was that they did not attract the wrong kind of attention from the gangs that now ran these streets. The whole city trembled in fear.

Uncle Gene sighed and shook his head slightly as he and Jonathan made their way through the market.

"What is it, Uncle?" Jonathan asked with concern in his voice. Jonathan thought Gene had seen some warning signs of danger. Over the years, Jonathan had come to trust Uncle Gene's powers of observation, especially when it came to people. Uncle Gene had told Jonathan that reading people was Gene's spiritual gift.

Gene smiled at Jonathan. "Oh, nothing but an old man's surfacing memories. Coming to the market used to be a celebration between communities, a social gathering that made us stronger. Now it is just a gathering of individuals permeated by suspicion and fear.

"It all changed when criminals were no longer held accountable for their actions. When our government, to further their self-centered delusions of grandeur, began to blame the police and law-abiding citizens for the ills of society instead of blaming those that preyed on society," Gene said through gritted teeth.

It was very seldom that Jonathan saw Uncle Gene get angry; however, when he spoke of the evil that had destroyed his country, the old man's fires lit and burned bright.

"I am sorry, Jonathan, I still cannot stand the evil that has taken over this country. I pray every day that I can forgive those who did this, and I do forgive them, but the evil behind it must be hated by Christians and opposed at every turn."

"You speak of Satan, don't you, Uncle Gene?" Jonathan asked.

"Yes, my boy, I do indeed."

"How do we separate the people that do these things and the evil? I guess what I am asking is, 'How do we forgive those who have done these things to all of us?' I thought if anyone didn't have trouble forgiving, it would be you, Uncle Gene."

Uncle Gene gave Jonathan a derisive smile and a light rap on the back of his head.

"Oh, my boy, do not put me on such a high pedestal. I am flawed and broken just like everyone else. The difference is my Lord and Savior Jesus lives within me. His holy spirit guides me, counsels me, and disciplines me. I am not able to forgive because of me. I can forgive because He forgives me and out of love for Him. I follow what He tells me and all of us to do. Forgive others."

"But there is still a struggle there," asked Jonathan.

Uncle Gene rubbed his eyes and answered, "Of course, Satan is always trying to trip up Christians into doing the wrong things for the wrong reasons. If he can get us to do that, then it damages our witness to the rest of the world that Jesus is Lord of all."

Jonathan nodded his head in understanding. "So when we do bad things or even do not forgive, it pushes people away from Christ instead of toward Him?"

Uncle Gene raised a thumb in the air and said, "Exactly."

"Uncle Gene, if you could give one piece of advice to anyone about forgiveness, what would it be?"

Uncle Gene smiled. "Oh, that is an easy one. There but by the grace of God go I. If not for Jesus and the salvation that He gifted me, that would be me doing those evil things. That could be me destroying the country through greed and fearmongering, that could be me killing and robbing my fellow man, that could be me lost in a sea of my own filth and debauchery.

"Always remember, Jonathan, who saved you and me and the price He paid. Therefore, whenever I begin to get full of myself, I am reminded of who to give praise to by King David. In Psalms 47:6–7, he says, 'Sing praises to God, sing praises; sing praises to our King, sing praises. For God is the King of all the earth; sing to Him a psalm of praise.'"

Jonathan took the chiding in good humor. Uncle Gene was always teaching, always praising God, and always asking not to be elevated above anyone else. Even though Uncle Gene was the leader of their little merry band of believers, he never put on airs or lorded over any of them. He would gently discipline those who needed it, just as he had with Jonathan just now, but somehow when Uncle spoke to him about something that needed correcting in his behavior, he not only felt the sting of it but also felt the joy and love of it.

"Thank you, oh lowly servant," Jonathan said in a sarcastic and humor-filled tone.

Gene turned his head toward Jonathan and opened his mouth to chide him again, then he saw the impish grin on Jonathan's face, then he just started laughing.

As they continued to walk and as the ringing quality of Uncle Gene's laughter began to fade, a young man of perhaps late teens stepped in front of Uncle Gene.

"Hey, you, old man," he said in an insulting and grating tone.

Jonathan immediately began to step in front of Uncle Gene to protect him. Jonathan's fist began to clinch. Uncle Gene gently placed his arm in front of Jonathan and held him in place; the old man was stronger than he looked.

Gene looked at the young man and said, "Yes, young man," allowing only the slightest sarcastic emphasis of the words young man. "May I help you in some way?"

"Yeah, did I just hear you talking about God?"

Uncle Gene eyed the young man and evaluated him through keen observation and the gift that God had granted him. Gene sighed.

The young man was perhaps seventeen years old. He was dressed in torn jeans, not the kind of tears from wear but the kind the kids wore these days. He wore a T-shirt that had a rude gesture plastered on the front and a blue jacket. His hair was brown, his face dirty, but with a sharpness to it. If he had to guess, Uncle Gene would say Western European descent. His eyes were brown as well and wide. There was fear on his face and in his voice. He was not sure about what he was doing. This young man could yet be saved; however, he was not ready to hear just yet. God had not prepared him to hear Gene's message. Gene must let the young man know he was a source of that message and intrigue the young man just enough to be curious.

"Why do you ask? You do not seek knowledge or wisdom of the Most High, you seek to ensnare, trap, and profit by causing pain to others. When you truly are seeking, come ask again, and I will tell you what you need to know."

"I know what I heard old man," the young man spat.

Uncle Gene turned a steely blue-eyed gaze upon the young man. "And yet you know nothing. This is truly the saddest part of your life."

The young man was stunned by this, and when he recovered, he looked up to see Jonathan smiling at him. Jonathan couldn't help it; he had been on the receiving end of Uncle Gene's biting insights. The young man lunged at Jonathan and shot a right fist toward Jonathan's face.

Uncle Gene intercepted the fist and gave the young man a quick jab to the nose that staggered him. The young man, seeing that he was not dealing with an easy prey, ran off down one of the side alleys.

As the young man ran away, some people glanced at the altercation. Most people just kept walking not wanting to become involved. A reality that had crept into this society was that people were either too afraid or just didn't care enough to step in. Some reached for their cell phones to record. After all, everyone in this warped society knew that if you wanted your fifteen minutes of fame, you had to be ready to capture either controversy or violence.

Jonathan's face was shocked. "Uncle Gene, I thought we were supposed to turn the other cheek, not bloody someone's nose."

"You see most people assume that because Christians are taught to be peaceful, forgive, and turn the other cheek, we will not protect ourselves or those we love. Nothing could be further from the truth. A good shepherd protects his flock, my boy. Had he struck me, I would have attempted to turn the other cheek, but he struck at you. Therefore, I was free to act to protect one of my own."

"Then why didn't you let me protect you when he insulted you?"

"Because it was an attack of words and a very poor one at that, but you were going to put hands on him and that would mean that you assaulted him first and you would have been in the wrong. As I said, a good shepherd protects his flock. Besides age and rank having privileges, the young man was a pompous popping jay, and the best thing for him at that moment was to pop the popping jay."

Jonathan laughed slightly and then said, "Uncle Gene, did you just make a joke about hitting someone?"

Uncle Gene smiled and looked at his young Christian brother, "Now, Jonathan, would I ever do something like that? Honestly, a man of my years joking about fisticuffs. Really?"

Uncle Gene gave Jonathan a wry smile and winked at him. "Enough of this, let's go meet Kyle. I hear he has strawberries, and you know they are my favorite."

# CHAPTER 4

## *The Abduction*

Kyle Strom was a short, portly man. His thinning gray-streaked brown hair somehow gave him a gnomish look. His brown eyes were clouding over from age, but he was a long-time friend of Gene's and a fellow brother in Christ. He owned a stall at the market, and he specialized in fruits and vegetables. As he saw the two approaching, he waved and had a huge grin spread across his ample face.

Kyle was one of the most joyful men you would ever want to meet. The Lord had blessed him with the ability to make anyone feel special. He always had a kind word and was quick with his wit and advice.

"Gene, Jonathan, it is good to see you two scoundrels again. Come, come, let me hear all about your days. Although, some of it I saw even from over here. You going into the fighting game, Gene? A little late in life, but my money is all on you, my friend."

Kyle huffed a laugh at his little dig at his friend.

Gene smiled, and as he approached the stall, he extended his hand, and the two men shook hands. "I think that was my one and only bout for a while. Good thing too. I would not want to be responsible for making you a rich man."

Kyle shook Jonathan's hand and asked, "What is the matter with you, Jonathan? Can't you keep this man from finding trouble?"

Jonathan smiled and said, "It is a cross I must bear, and it is not easy. Truth be told, though, I went to hit that jerk first, but Uncle Gene stopped me. If you ask me, it was so he could hit him."

Uncle Gene feigned a hurt expression, "Are you two quite done?"

The two men glanced at each other.

"Are we done, Jonathan?" asked Kyle.

Jonathan laughed and said, "No, but we can put it on hold until later."

"Fair enough," Kyle said. "Now what can I do for two of my favorite customers?"

Gene smiled slyly and looked up at his friend. "Well, rumor has it that you may just have some strawberries on hand. If you do, I would be willing to buy them, just so they don't go to waste mind you."

Kyle turned his head as he walked behind the counter of his stall and shook his finger at Gene. "Do not try to play like you do not love strawberries, my friend, I know better."

Kyle turned and started to gather up the supplies that the two men had come for.

Gene just inclined his head in acknowledgment and paused a moment to take in his surroundings.

The sounds of people hustling and bustling, going about their business were there, but what always struck Gene these days was the absence of conversation. The conversation that Kyle, Jonathan, and he just had was the most Gene had heard since they entered the alley. Oh, the place was crowded, and there were shouts of anger and complaint, but there was no exchange of pleasantries, no hellos, or goodbyes, and no "how is the family."

The whole place seemed devoid of courtesy and kindness. Gene had to wonder if this was part of what made Jesus angry when He drove the merchants and money changers out of the temple. There was no compassion and no love, just greed and hate. The only time that the Bible tells us that Jesus got angry was when he drove the merchants and money exchangers out of the temple.

Gene wondered, *Was it lying and cheating? Was it the lack of love and compassion?*

Then he understood, it was both. By exhibiting these loathsome behaviors in the temple, these men were defiling God's house. Instead of a place where men should come to share and rejoice with God, the place had become a place to worship money and things. Instead of a place where men should share openly and lovingly, it had become a place to exhibit greed and cheat your fellow man.

Therefore, Jesus grew angry and drove the men out. However, Jesus still loved them. He could have just ended their lives, but He had compassion and still gave them a chance to accept Him as Lord and Savior. Jesus told us to love our enemies. He knew that no matter how bad the sin or offense was, we must love them so that we can witness to them and allow them to accept Him.

In his mind, Gene prayed, *Lord, I have forgiven people. I have witnessed people. Why are You reminding me of this now?*

*Soon,* came the response.

Gene shook his head in understanding and sadness. Jonathan placed a hand on Uncle Gene's shoulder and stared at him in concern.

Gene smiled. "Ah, boy, do not frown. You will look older than I do in a week if you keep that up."

"I worry about you, Uncle Gene. You have had more and more of those moments recently. Moments where you just seem to slip away. Where do you go?"

Uncle Gene nodded. "The Holy Spirit speaks, He reveals, He teaches, He reassures, He disciplines, and He loves. This is where I am at. I am having things revealed to me, and I am having things made clearer. God has a plan for all of us. God protects us and shows us what we must do in this life. I do not know where God is taking me next, but a change is coming, and I feel it is vital that I be ready for it."

Kyle returned with two heavily laden bags and plopped them down on the counter, giving a little grunt of exertion as he did.

Gene and Jonathan's eyes widened as they looked upon the bounty of goods. "This is not what we ordered, my friend, this is five times the amount. We cannot afford this, how, why."

Kyle put up a hand to stop the protests and said, "This is from the community of Christian merchants here. There are not many of us, but we each contributed to your community's needs. There is no charge for any of this. We know the good you are doing, my friend, and we have been led to give you this as a gift from God, including these."

Kyle reached into one of the burlap sacks and withdrew some of the most beautiful strawberries Gene had ever seen.

Gene just stared in awe. Jonathan exclaimed, "Wow."

Gene reached out his hand and took three of the gorgeous berries. He put two of them in his coat pocket. The third he held just under his nose and breathed deeply taking in the enticing aroma of a perfectly ripe strawberry.

The two men looked curiously at Uncle Gene. He had never taken any food for himself first; he had always insisted that the community get first dibs on all the supplies.

"Uncle Gene, are you okay?" Jonathan asked. "You have never taken first dibs on anything."

Uncle Gene stood there with the strawberry in his hand and said, "This one is a gift for me. The other two are gifts for others. Now you must go, Jonathan. Take the supplies back to the camp and prepare the others to move. You will lead them now. God had used me to prepare you for this, so do not worry or be afraid, but you must go now."

Jonathan instinctively picked up two bags and draped them over his shoulders. He had followed Uncle Gene's orders for a long time, so it took a moment before he even allowed himself to question what was going on.

"Uncle Gene, what are you talking about? If we must go, you must come with me. Whatever it is we can figure it out once we get back to camp."

Uncle Gene turned and placed his hand on the face of his beloved brother Jonathan. A look of immense pride and joy brightened his blue eyes. "No, my boy, you must go, and I must stay. Our paths separate for a time here. God has different tasks for us now, yours lies with our community, mine is elsewhere."

"No!" Jonathan shouted. "I go where you go. I…"

"Not this time Jonathan, you must go. If you love the Lord and you love me, you have to leave now."

There was no anger in Gene's voice, but there was command. He left no doubt that Jonathan was to follow his command.

Jonathan was in anguish. His mentor, his brother, and his spiritual father had just given him a command, one that he knew came from God, but his loyalty to his friend was in combat with his willingness to follow God's command.

*What am I supposed to do?* he thought.

"Jonathan," Gene said in a calm and peaceful voice. "You do not serve me, you serve God. Do not heed what man tells you. Heed what God tells you. What does God tell you now?"

Jonathan bowed his head and prayed. When his head came back up, he looked at Uncle Gene with tears in his eyes, but his voice was firm. "I am to leave." The two men touched foreheads in a farewell. He knew his life would never be the same as he took his first steps on a new journey God had for him.

As Jonathan left, Gene bit into the strawberry. It was sweet and tart, and the two flavors burst onto his tongue as the juice ran down his chin. He stood there for a moment and just savored the gift God had given him. Once he had finished, he looked up to see Kyle staring dumbfounded at him.

Kyle handed Gene a napkin. "Here, wipe your face. What in the heck was that all about? You just sent Jonathan away, and you're staying here? What is here for you? Go be with your people. They need you. We need you out there with them."

Gene shook his head slowly. "Not anymore, it is Jonathan's time now. The Lord has another task for me, one that I will covet your prayers for, so I ask you to leave and get all our brothers and sisters who are here to leave as well. You cannot be here anymore."

Kyle's face grew red in anger. "I will not abandon…" As Kyle looked at Gene's face and saw the peace in it, the acceptance, and the pure joy that only comes from God, he stopped speaking. It was as if someone at punched him in the gut. He did not have any air to continue his tirade. As Kyle closed his shop and began to leave, he put a hand on Gene's shoulder and said, "You are always in my prayers, brother, go with God."

Gene patted his friend on his shoulder and said, "You as well."

Gene stood there for a time and then started to walk around the market. God only had revealed to him that he was to send Jonathan and Kyle away from him, that his path took a different turn here. So when he heard, "That's him there," Gene did not realize that he was him in that statement until he saw the face of the young man he had confronted earlier.

*Ah, Lord, You do have a way about You*, Gene thought as five men rushed him and began to beat him into submission. Gene did not fight back. First, he did not stand a chance against five younger opponents, and second Gene knew that this was where God wanted Him to go.

The sounds of whooshing bats and thumping flesh followed by grunts of pain went on for what seemed like forever, but the five had Gene down quickly.

Then through the ringing in Gene's ear, he heard a guttural, oily-sounding voice say, "Bring the old man. If he is who I think he is he is worth some coin, if not we can always have some fun with him."

Gene tried to get up, but despite knowing the Lord wanted him to go, he did not wish to go. The last thought before a swift blow was, *Lord, why, so often, does sharing Your love have to be so painful?* Then unconsciousness followed.

# CHAPTER 5

## *The New Reality*

One eye fluttered open, the other tried to follow suit, but it did not open wide, and the effort to open it was painful. So his right eye was swollen almost shut, his head still rang like a church bell on Easter Sunday, and his hands were bound. Other than that, Gene was perfectly fine. He sat up and pushed his back up against a wall. This made him somewhat more comfortable and gave him a better look at his surroundings.

The light in the place was distant and dim. However, he could tell that he was in a warehouse. The concrete floor was cold to the touch. The steel girders along the walls and ceiling spoke of a cavernous building. Rain pinged off a metal roof, and some holes in the roof were obvious as some of the rain splatted onto the concrete floor. Flickering neon lights streamed in through high windows near the ceiling.

If he had to guess, he was somewhere down by the river docks. He could not hear the river over the rain, but he could detect a smell of old fish and grease.

He saw large double doors on the opposite wall, and he pushed with his legs and stood up with the help of the wall. As the world seemed to tumble over itself; Gene thought, maybe that wasn't such a good idea. However, his instincts told him that if he had a chance to escape, he had to risk it.

Some steps were a stumble, and some were solid. He imagined he looked like one of the zombies in those old movies. As he started to laugh at his own joke, his head reminded him that nothing was humorous right now. The wave of pain almost brought him down, but he stopped, took a breath, and pushed onto the door.

Gene went to the door. It was one of those large steel double doors. The kind that you open from the middle, and it slides to either side. He grabbed the middle handles of the door and the world flipped in dizziness. He gave himself a moment to allow his equilibrium to stop, trying to tell him his falling down a deep dark hole; then he gave a tug on the door. Nothing happened. He looked through a small crack in the middle of the door and could see the hasp of a padlock on the other side.

Well, he thought, I guess that would have been way too easy. Now he was beginning to feel the other injuries his body had sustained. His ribs ached and throbbed. His cheekbone was swollen and was competing for the number one spot of pain on the list. His back felt like someone had jumped up and down on it, and he really had to pee.

Gene looked around and saw back where he had come from a bucket. He walked back over to where the bucket was and by the smell, he confirmed the bucket was indeed intended to be used as his facility.

*Well, at least they have provided for some convenience,* he mused.

He relieved himself and was surprised at just how much better he felt afterward.

The sound of a door opening on the far end of the warehouse reached his ears, and light flashed for a moment from that direction. Gene heard footsteps coming his way. Gene moved back over to where he had woken up and slid back down the wall.

He did not know what to expect, but it was probably not going to be good. So Gene slumped his head onto his chest and feigned unconsciousness. The steps grew closer, there were at least three men, and they spoke as they came closer.

"What do you expect to do with this old man? He does not seem like anything special," asked the first voice. It was the oily-voiced man he had seen in the market.

A second voice, deeper with a much more evil growl in it, answered, "You are an idiot. This man is wanted by the authorities, but before we turn him over, we are going to find out where his followers are, and when he gives them up, we will find them, turn them in, and the authorities will pay us and owe us a favor. Not to mention that they will see our little group here as loyal to the powers that be and leave us to do what we please to this part of the city."

A third voice, Gene thought it sounded like the younger man that initially confronted him said, "Yeah, idiot, don't you know anyt—" The voice stopped abruptly and was cut off by a loud slapping sound and a whimper of pain.

"Rat, you may have found him, but that does not give you the right to speak, shut your mouth." It was the gravelly voice again.

Obviously, the one in charge, Gene thought.

The three men approached and stood in front of Gene, looking down at him.

"Bah, the old man is still out. He may even be dead," the first voice spoke.

"Again, you prove yourself to be an idiot Sloan. He is awake."

"How can you tell?" said the younger voice.

The one in charge gave the young man a harsh look but decided against hitting him again.

"Well, there may be hope for you Benny. At least you ask a pertinent question."

The younger one, evidently known as Benny nodded and stayed quiet and still.

"Look at his breathing, the rate at which his chest rises and falls, that is the respiration of a man who is conscious. Also, his hands are clenched. He is listening to us right now, aren't you, old man?"

Gene raised his head slowly. He looked the leader in the eyes. The man was about twenty-eight or thirty. He was six foot five inches tall and probably weighed somewhere above two hundred and fifty pounds. He was dressed all in black, black jeans, a black shirt, socks, and shoes. His face had an ugly scar across his forehead, but other than that, his features were very pleasant to look at. His nose was long and chiseled, and his jawline was aquiline. His face was all sharp lines and angles, and it did not match his large muscular frame. It made him look more sinister somehow.

However, what gave Gene the most pause was that when he looked into the brown eyes of his adductor; he saw intelligence there, not just street smarts, but book learning as well. Gene knew that this person was more dangerous because he was using his God-given abilities for evil; he was using the people that he had under his sway as his army. Gene gave a shudder.

The tall man smiled, a smile that did not reflect in his eyes. He thought Gene's shudder was one of fear. It was not, it was one of revulsion.

The one known as Sloan asked, "What are we going to do with him, Aaron?"

The one knew evidently as Aaron backhanded Sloan and shouted, "Since he is awake, give him food and water, as I told you before buffoon!"

Aaron turned his gaze back to Gene. "Enjoy, it will be the last you have for a while. Tomorrow, we will get the information we need from you, so enjoy tonight because the rest of your time here will not be as pleasant."

The three men turned and walked away. Benny and Sloan argued about who was going to bring the old man his dinner, pushing and shoving ensued until Aaron slapped both just as they slammed the door shut and left Gene in dimly lit relative silence.

In the distance, Gene could hear horns honking and tires rumbling on the highways, even some aircraft flying overhead. It was like the sounds he sometimes heard in a dream or when he stood in the hills surrounding their camp, there and then not, fading in and out, teasingly close, and yet so far away.

Gene got up and began to look for any means of escape. There was very little light, so he had to mainly rely on his sense of direction and touch. From what he could tell, he was in an old warehouse, but it was locked up tight. He also could tell from the sounds outside that he was not in the city but somewhere just outside of it.

He found the door that the three men had exited. They had been careful to lock it as they left. So no escape was coming from that direction. He made the circuit around the warehouse three times, just to be sure he had not missed anything and so he could familiarize himself with the layout.

He was in a long rectangular warehouse. Steel girders spaced every twelve feet ran from a thick concrete floor to large steel rafters, or at least he assumed this because he could not actually see the ceiling very well. This place had not been built anytime soon; it had been a while since buildings were built entirely out of steel. However, much to Gene's annoyance, the building was still very solid and very locked. There were not even any windows in the place. If this place had been underground, it would have made an excellent bomb shelter.

During his exploring, Gene had found a table and chair not far from where he had awoken. He sat down in the chair, folded his hands, bowed his head, and began to pray.

"Oh, Father, this is not good. I am scared, I am worried, and I am anxious, Father. I am scared for myself, I am worried about my brothers and sisters, and I am anxious about these men that I find myself in the midst of. Please, Lord, deliver me from the evil men and let me go back to my flock." Gene sighed and continued, "However, Father, not my will but Your will be done."

"Father God, please protect my brothers and sisters. Lord, I lift my captors, and I pray that they will come to know Your love. I pray that they will accept You as Lord and Savior of their lives. This world has become a cesspool of evil and debauchery, yet you still love all of us, Lord, and desire that we would come to you. Help them, oh Jesus, to come to know You. In Jesus's name, I pray. Amen."

Once Gene had finished his prayer, he laid his head down, and he found himself slipping into sleep. Just before sleep claimed him, he heard a calm.

A strong, loving voice said, "Peace."

Sometime later, Gene did not know how long he had been asleep. He was rudely awakened by a kick to the ribs. A whoosh of air escaped his lungs, as he was knocked out of the chair and skidded across the concrete floor. He sat up quickly; his hands coming up in a defensive posture.

Before him, holding a bowl and bottled water was Sloan. The man was pudgy, and his face was plump and red as if he was constantly angry. His eyes were blue, his nose looked as if it had been broken too many times, his hair was long to his shoulders, and it was straggly and greasy-looking. He stood about five foot nine inches tall, and he had not washed himself in some time judging by the smell.

"The boss said to feed you, so here is your food." Sloan sat the food and water on the concrete floor in front of Gene. He slammed it on the floor so that some of the contents of the bowl spilled over. He glared at Gene with hatred and then said, "Don't know why we are wasting food on you. You know what is coming, old man? We are going to beat the snot out of you until you tell us what we want to know. You can save yourself some trouble and just tell us where your community of lunatics lives."

Gene relaxed his hands and reached for the bowl of food. It was some type of vegetable soup. There was no spoon, so Gene picked up the bowl and began to sip its contents. It was not seasoned and some of the vegetables were on the verge of going bad, but Gene knew he needed to keep his strength up, so he ate.

As he sipped at his soup, Sloan continued to glare at him. The man held his anger like an old miserable friend.

"I am not afraid," said Gene in a calm voice. "My Lord and Savior Jesus Christ is with me, and I do not fear what you can do with this body. My only concern is for those of my community and you and your companions."

Sloan laughed. "You concerned for us? Liar!" Sloan screamed and slapped Gene hard across his face. The bowl of soup went flying out of Gene's hands, and a trickle of blood ran down his chin from a split lip.

Gene wiped his chin and lip, looked at Sloan, and offered the other cheek for him to slap. "As I said, young man, I do not fear you. Would it make you feel better to slap me again? Do you think it would take your pain away? If so, I offer you my face as a salve."

"A what? You are a crazy old man, and you should be afraid. I have seen what Aaron can do when he means business, and the amount of pay we would get for bringing you and your crazies in would keep us well-provisioned for at least a year. As far as this Lord of yours, I don't see anyone else in this warehouse but us."

Gene raised his hand again to slap Gene but stopped. "Bah, you ain't worth it. You will get yours soon enough." With a string of curse words that would make a sailor blush, Sloan walked away.

"Thank You for giving me the courage and peace to not lash out at him." Gene shook his head and thought, *Oh, Lord, there is a lot of anger in that one. Please give his heart peace and let him let go of all that hatred. I am not capable of loving these jerks, I am not able to stop myself from hating them, but You are more than capable of giving me what I need to love them and tell them about You. I pray in Jesus's name. Amen.*"

For some time, Gene had been aware that when he prayed, God would answer his prayers as God saw fit. After all, God's will is always better than Gene's will.

Gene had also noticed that when he prayed for strength, patience, understanding, or peace, soon after Satan would soon try to undermine Gene's faith and try to strip away the gifts that God had already given Gene. In his youth, it had been easy for Satan to strip these gifts away. All Satan had to do was make Gene angry or have the world pile on even more obstacles and distractions and Gene would focus on the wrong things.

Over the years, God had taught Gene how to focus on God and not the world. Gene had just prayed for the man who had hit him, Sloan, was his name. Gene had asked God to forgive him and to reach Sloan. So of course, Gene's temptation of ending the man's life was what Satan attacked him with. Many years ago, Gene had learned how to defend himself. He had taken martial arts, learned to wield swords, and even had an extensive gun collection and had been trained in the use of firearms.

Right now, all Gene could think of was how he could take Sloan out. How, if given the chance, he would kick the man in the chest, knock him down, swing up behind him, get him in a choke hold, and snap his neck. These thoughts brought a smile to Gene's lips. It was as his lips spread into a smile that Gene stopped himself from fantasizing about killing Sloan.

Gene chastised himself. *Oh, Lord, I am sorry. Please forgive me for such thoughts. It is You who protect me*, he thought. *Please, Lord, let me out of here. How can I be a witness to people who are threatening to beat me and bring harm to my flock? I am not the right person for this. All I what to do is smash their faces in and escape.*

Gene sighed, as he prayed with all his heart. He had given his petition to the Lord. He drew in a breath and shuddered as the air filled his lungs. "But not my will but your will, Lord."

Gene picked up the bowl and water off the floor and sat back down at the table. Gene ate what was left of the soup and drank the water. Morning would come soon enough, and he would have to deal with whatever came.

He was afraid, but he knew he was not alone. He laid down on the concrete floor, and as he struggled to fall back asleep, he heard the Holy Spirit say to him, *Peace*. He soon was asleep.

# CHAPTER 6

## *Pursuit*

This had to be the toughest thing that God had ever asked Jonathan to do—to leave Uncle Gene when he knew trouble was maddening. Jonathan had just made it around the corner when he heard the sounds of a struggle. Uncle Gene, he thought, turned to go back, turned back around to obey what God had instructed him to do, and then he just froze in place. Jonathan heard someone say, bring the old man and the word coin. Jonathan was in anguish; he wanted and needed to go help his friend, mentor, and spiritual father, but God had told him to leave. Jonathan did the only thing that he knew to do.

He prayed, "Father, please let me go to Uncle Gene. Let me help him."

Tears of frustration and fear ran down Jonathan's face as he added, "But not my will, Father, but your will. In Jesus's name. I pray."

As soon as Jonathan finished his prayer, a calm, peaceful, loving voice answered, *"Follow only."*

Jonathan stumbled in shock for a moment. God had never spoken directly to him, not like this. He knew the presence of the Holy Spirit and the guidance when he got a word from God, but God had just spoken directly to him.

*Wow*, he thought and, in a stammered, breathy, barely audible voice, replied, "Yes, Father, th…thank you."

Jonathan's legs had been wobbly and weak, but now he had plenty of strength and he whirled and sprinted back to the market. He saw Kyle just closing his shop and he stopped just in time not to take out the makeshift counter.

Jonathan opened his mouth to speak, and Kyle just pointed. "They went that away."

"I am to follow them," Jonathan managed to get out.

"I know," came Kyle's reply. "They went that away, but do not get too close to the young one. They will be watching for anyone that follows."

Jonathan nodded even as he turned and pursued those who had taken his friend.

Jonathan had caught up to the group soon after he started his pursuit. He stayed well back as he did not want to be discovered. God had told him to follow only. He was trying to obey, even though every part of him wanted to catch them and beat them senselessly and rescue Uncle Gene.

As he followed, he couldn't help but admire the group's knowledge of the ruined city. They took a circuitous route through the ruins that kept them, for the most part, out of sight. They walked at a brisk but even pace through rumble, broken walls, and mounds of concrete and steel. Whoever was leading them knew the city very well.

Several times along the way, Jonathan had to duck or dive behind cover as they had someone near the rear of the group looking for pursuit of any kind. Jonathan was sure that he had been spotted at least twice, but the lookout never raised the alarm, and the Holy Spirit indicated to him to continue to follow. Jonathan was scared, but he would trust God, no matter what came.

It was getting dark, and the rubble of the streets was hazardous to navigate even during the daylight hours. Jonathan was young and agile, but even he stumbled and fell into this maze of debris. More than once, he had to stifle a yelp of pain as his knees and hands to the brute of abuse. Also, he was pretty sure that he had impaled his hand on a piece of rebar at one point during his pursuit. He tore a piece of his shirt and wrapped it quickly.

As he moved through the shadows, Jonathan noticed occasionally that others moved in the shadows as well. Most were hooded and dressed in dark clothes. Some moved with stealth as he did, while others were loud banging and clanging, even screaming in anguish and despair. For a moment, he was afraid that maybe they were lookouts for the group he followed. However, as he observed them, he could tell that were just beaten down, sad people, looking for whatever they could salvage in this desolate place.

Jonathan realized after half an hour that they were moving toward the old docks. Towering rusty old cranes filled the skyline. Abandoned warehouses lined the broken concrete avenues. Of course, Jonathan thought, this is the perfect place. Hardly anyone is going to hear anything you do to a person here, and if by chance, there is someone who hears, they are not going to get involved. This area was not exactly what one would call a good part of town. Even when the city was still civilized, this part of the city was home to the worst kind of people.

Jonathan took a chance to get closer now. There were plenty of buildings to duck behind and lots of shadows to melt away in. He saw the group drag Uncle Gene into one of the bigger warehouses. Huge double doors that slid horizontally along steel rails allowed access to the building.

Uncle Gene's body was still limp, he had yet to wake up from being knocked unconscious, or at least, Jonathan hoped he was just unconscious. Surely, Uncle Gene was still alive. The group would not have drug a dead man all this way.

Jonathan positioned himself about fifty feet away from the door. He was hidden behind a crumbled wall of another warehouse. He was not in front of the door to the other warehouse, but he had a good view of it. Several people came and went as he watched. After about fifteen minutes or so went by, he could see that the door had been locked, and two guards stood outside the doors.

The guards were not particularly alert as they were just to keep what was in the building from escaping. They did not think that anyone else would be foolish enough to attempt to rescue some old man.

However, that was exactly what Jonathan had in mind. He would find a way. Surely God would provide a way.

Jonathan waited another five minutes just to be sure that no one was coming back. He backed away from his hiding spot putting distance between himself and the front door where the guards stood. Making sure he was far enough away, he made his way around the warehouse that held his friend. Once he was in the shadow of the building, he made his way to the concrete and steel walls of the warehouse and carefully began making his way around it. He had to find another way in. He had to find a way to get Uncle Gene out of his captor's hands.

Jonathan crept around the building. Each footfall was measured, each breath taken deliberately and slowly. Some of the rubble had been removed from around the walls of the warehouse but not all. Jonathan had to move with care as he searched for another entrance to the monstrosity of a building. Oddly enough, there was not another entrance except the large sliding metal doors at the front which were being guarded. It was time to come up with another plan.

Jonathan had been in worse places and smelled worse parts of the city, but not by much. Living in the countryside and the fresh air had lessened Jonathan's ability to ignore the smells of the city. Jonathan realized that he had lost his city boy nose. The good thing about its loss was that he now smelled everything. He was no longer immune to the grotesque smells of his surroundings, so he followed his nose. If he could not gain entrance above ground perhaps, he could find a way below ground. He smelled a sewer line somewhere nearby. If he could find it, maybe there were large enough pipes and drains that he could gain entrance to the warehouse that way.

It did not take long for him to locate the manhole cover. It was behind the building, so there was very little chance that the guards would see him. However, the cover was heavy, and it would take some effort to open it without making any noise.

Jonathan was wiry, but he was strong. However, moving something heavy slowly to not make noise is hard. After five minutes of prying, lifting, and shimming the cover, Jonathan's brow was beading sweat from his exertions.

He finally got the cover removed. Jonathan took his small penlight from his pocket. He remembered when Uncle Gene had insisted that he start carrying the device.

"Why do I need this?" he had asked. "We have lights in the cave."

Uncle Gene had given him that Uncle Gene smile, patient yet sarcastic in nature. Uncle Gene then replied, "Boy, you live in a cave. What if the lights go out?"

Jonathan had ducked his head and said, "Ah, good point."

Uncle Gene had patted him on his head and said, "See you can be taught."

Like most of Uncle Gene's lessons, it was given with love and joy in his voice. So much so that you did not feel bad about making a mistake, rather you felt good about having learned something.

Jonathan shined the light down the hole. A ladder led down to brackish water which smelled exactly how he remembered sewers smelling foul. He did not know what could be down there, and he did not want to go down into a dark stinky hole, but if it meant finding a way to get Uncle Gene out of that warehouse, it was worth the discomfort and risk.

Some parts of the rungs of the ladder were slimy, and other parts were crusty. Jonathan didn't want to think about either sensation. However, when he jumped down the last five feet to the bottom, he wished for the ladder again. The water had not been disturbed in years, and as his feet splashed down, the cold of the water made him inhale a sharp breath. That was when the stench, which he thought was bad before, made him gag. For several minutes, he just stood there trying not to hurl up the entire contents of his stomach.

Slowly, he adjusted to his surroundings. The water he had landed in came up to just above his knees. He shined the light around the pipes and saw that they ran toward the warehouse and away. Of course, he started walking slowly toward the warehouse. Jonathan guessed that he was a good four hundred yards from the building that held Uncle Gene. Each step brought a fresh wave of putrid odors to his nose. His eyes watered from the stench, and he constantly had to remind his stomach that he was in charge.

Tiny feet scurried along the walls and ceiling, and when he did shine his light in that direction, he wished that he hadn't. Rats just glared at him like the intruder he was, and they were none too happy with this interloper.

A few times Jonathan could have sworn that something brushed past his feet and legs. He tried not to think about what it might have been.

An eternity later, or what seemed like it, he saw a pipe above his head. Dim light shown through a grate in what he assumed was a floor. It was a smaller pipe than the one he stood in, but he thought it was big enough to allow him to squirm up into it. The pipe was a good three feet above his head and went on for another twenty feet or so. The problem was going to be gaining access without alerting any others to his presence.

It was then that he heard voices from above. They were feint and they carried an echoey quality to them. Jonathan listened hard. He did not recognize the first voice he heard, but he could not mistake the soft gravelly voice of his spiritual father. He had found where they had Uncle Gene.

Jonathan knew he could not get to Uncle Gene right now. He needed a way to ascend the tube that led into the warehouse. He needed a way to get through the grate in the floor above, and most of all, he needed backup if he was caught, a distraction to allow him to get Uncle Gene out. As much as he hated to admit it, he had to go back to camp, he needed help.

"Uncle Gene, I will be back for you," he whispered in the dark. "Lord, please keep him safe and speed my return."

Jonathan moved as fast as he could, and each second was a lifetime. His friend, his brother in Christ, was in deep trouble. He had to save him.

# CHAPTER 7

## *Coffee and Torture*

The door on the opposite side of the warehouse banged open. Gene was startled awake by the noise and opened his eyes with a snap of eyelids. He pushed himself off the cold concrete floor and slowly stood up. He was not a spring chicken anymore, and it took some time for the old body to mobilize, he thought as he sat down at the table.

He looked across the expanse of the warehouse and saw the same three men he had seen last night coming toward him, that's when it dawned on him, lights had been turned on. Large fixtures hung from the ceiling, each holding what must have been a two-hundred-watt bulb. After the darkness of the previous night, Gene's eyes took a moment to adjust. When they did, he confirmed that the three heading toward him were, Aaron, Sloan, and Benny.

They walked with more purpose this morning. They had things to accomplish today, Gene could see. As they got closer, Gene saw that Benny and Sloan were carrying equipment and Aaron was sipping on coffee and eating some type of breakfast sandwich. The smell of the coffee made Gene's mouth water.

He smiled. He loved his cup of morning coffee.

*Well*, he thought, *there can't be any harm in asking.*

"Coffee, I see you are like me. I love coffee in the morning. Would it be too much to ask if I may have some coffee?"

Aaron smiled. He gestured at Sloan. "Give the man his coffee," he instructed his lackey.

Sloan sat down on the equipment he was carrying, reached into a pouch in one of the backpacks, and pulled out a thermos of coffee. Steam poured out of the thermos as Sloan opened it. He gently poured coffee into a Styrofoam cup. He walked over to the table where Gene was sitting and set the cup in front of Gene.

As Gene leaned forward to grab the cup, Sloan grabbed the cup and, in one smooth motion, hurled the steaming contents into Gene's face.

Gene screamed in pain as his face was scalded with near-boiling liquid. His hands shot up to his face as he saw what Sloan was doing, but his reflexes were not as fast as they once had been, and most of the coffee had hit the mark.

His face felt like it was on fire, his eyes had slammed shut, and only a little of the hot liquid had gotten into his eyes. His cheeks and forehead, he could feel, were already forming painful blisters, and he now had second and third-degree burns on his face.

As Gene continued to scream and writhe in agony, he heard Sloan tell Aaron, "Coffee has been served, sir."

Gene heard Aaron chuckle. "You are one sick puppy, Sloan."

"That is a compliment coming from you," Sloan said with a bow and evil grin.

Gene heard Aaron drag up another chair. His screams had become muffled grunts of pain. When Gene could see again, he saw Aaron sitting at the opposite end of the table.

Aaron grinned, a grin that had malice in it, a grin that did not reach his eyes. "Well, now that you have had your morning Joe, we are ready to get started."

Gene glared at the man and his fists clenched in anger. He wanted nothing more than to beat the living snot out of this filth of humanity. He prayed silently, "Lord, please allow me to teach these vermin a lesson they will never forget." His mind was suddenly at peace, and his pain subsided. The anger and hatred he felt melted away. *Peace* came into his mind and filled his whole being with the love and joy of Christ.

*Well*, Gene thought, *looks like we are doing this the hard way. All right, Lord, Your will be done.*

Aaron saw the glare of anger and the clenched fists of hatred, and he smiled at Gene. "Well, it seems you do know how to hate. I thought Christians were supposed to love their enemies. Do you want to kill us old man? Do you want revenge on Sloan there? I tell you what, say the word and I will allow you to fight Sloan. If you beat him, I will let you go. What say you to that?"

As Aaron was speaking, he saw the anger and hatred leave Gene. His fists unclenched, and his face became tranquil. As Gene looked back at Aaron now, there was no fire only love and strength. Aaron could not believe what he was seeing. The man had just had scalding coffee thrown in his face, and after a momentary flash of anger, he sat there as if he were among friends.

Then the old man spoke, his voice was calm and even, and there was no bitterness or anger only peace and love.

"I do not wish to fight or harm anyone. My only wish is that I be allowed to leave."

Aaron made a sound of pfff and then said, "Ah man, for a moment, I thought you were going to rip Sloan to shreds. Then you went all passive and Zen. Are you a coward or just too old to fight?"

"Of course, Christians know anger and hatred. We are just as flawed as those who do not follow our Lord and Savior, Christ Jesus. The difference is that we know God's love and forgiveness. We have accepted Christ as our Savior, and in that moment, we are changed. We no longer live our lives for ourselves. We live for Christ. We are not able to love those who do us wrong because of ourselves but because of the love that God gives us. We can love and forgive those who do us harm because of God's love, and since we love Him, we follow what he asked us to do. As far as being a coward, ask yourself this question, 'What takes more courage? To pummel someone who has done you wrong or to love and forgive them even when they have hurt you?'"

Aaron pulled a length of rope from his pocket and began to wrap it around his right hand. "Well, if this was a debate in philosophy, that would be an interesting question and a good place to start the discussion. However, this is not a debate. This is a question-and-answer session. Meaning, I ask the questions and you answer them. Where are your people camped? You tell us that, and we will take you back to them."

As he had been talking, Aaron got up and walked to stand in front of Gene's place at the table. He now stood in front of Gene, and he leaned in trying to intimidate Gene.

"Why are you so keen to know where my camp is?" Gene asked. "We are of no great consequence. We are only trying to survive just like everyone else."

Aaron's fist lashed out and caught Gene in his left cheekbone with a quick jab of his rope-wound hand. The pain was instant, and Gene's head snapped back. A bruise was already forming by the time Gene gazed back into his captor's eyes. There was no mercy, only glee at being able to inflict harm on another.

All that Gene was holding onto at that moment was God's word, specifically Romans 5 verse 3.

"We also rejoice in our sufferings because suffering produces perseverance, perseverance, character; and character, hope." *Lord,* Gene thought, *give me hope through this. Otherwise, it was a waste of my face.*

Gene could not help himself; he chuckled at his mental joke.

"I told you, old man, I ask the questions here. Now where is your camp?"

Aaron saw the man chuckle, and he was outraged. "You think this is funny, old man?" Aaron was fast and strong; he began raining blow after blow down on Gene's head.

Gene's head went back and forth violently. His face went from a single bruise on his cheek to a myriad of matted flesh. In some places, blood trickled, and in others, it ran and spattered. Gene had taken worse and looked worse, but that had always been at the end of a fight. This one was just starting.

Everyone has a limit, a point, or a place where the brain says, "No more, we are checking out." When Gene hit his, Aaron saw that he was unconscious and stopped pummeling him.

Stupid Aaron thought, *If I kill the old fool, then I don't get a payday.*

He stepped back and hollered for Benny, "Benny, bring a bucket of water. Wake this worthless scum up."

Benny stepped forward with a two-gallon tin bucket and tossed the contents all over Gene's face and torso.

Gene returned quickly from the sweet oblivion of blackness. He was soaking wet, and the water stung his wounds, and some had gotten up his nose. He sputtered and coughed. Afterward, he straightened himself up and said, "Oh, it's still you."

Aaron had regained some of his composure and asked, "Who did you think it would be, God?"

Gene smiled, although he winced in pain as he did so, and said, "Why, yes, I thought it might be."

Aaron leaned close again. "Do you have a death wish, old man? Do all so-called Christians have a death wish?"

Gene stared at Aaron for a moment. "Death wish? No, we love life. We do not want to die. However, we are not afraid of death because we know what awaits us when we leave this mortal coil."

Aaron looked at Gene and laughed. "Fool, when you die, you don't go anywhere. You just cease to exist, and no amount of prayer or whatever else you have been brainwashed with is going to change that."

Aaron began to unwrap the rope from his hand. He gestured to Benny, and Benny came forward with a cart loaded down with a twelve-volt car battery and cables.

Gene shot a glance at the cart that Benny was bringing in. He swallowed hard, and his heart leaped out of his chest. How much of this could he endure? Panic began to grip him. *Peace* came the calm voice. It was not just in his head, it was in his being, and it filled him from top to bottom.

Gene lowered his head and whispered a prayer, "Thank You, Lord Jesus, thank You."

"Aaron—may I call you Aaron? I mean, after all, you are torturing me. That, I suppose, is a relationship. Can't call it friendship, but we are not strangers."

Aaron nodded his head. "Why sure, Gene, you can call me Aaron. Let's be civil as I fry your skin from your bones." Aaron began attaching the cables to the battery.

Gene internally winced as he saw sparks pop when Aaron made the connection of the cables. He looked at each man in the room and spoke.

"You all misunderstand. I do not pray today to get into heaven. I prayed that prayer a long time ago. Jesus forgave me of my sins, reconciled me with God the Father, and blessed me with His holy spirit, and since that day, my home in heaven has been assured. After we are saved by Christ, we do not have to pray for a place in His kingdom. Prayer is not an obligation so that we can obtain our place in heaven. As a matter of fact, the only thing we can do to get to heaven is submit ourselves to the mercy of the Father through Christ. All have sinned and fallen short of the righteousness of God. There is nothing that any man can do by himself that will gain him a place in God's kingdom. Only through submitting to Christ are we saved. We do this by asking Christ to be Lord over our lives, we submit ourselves to his will, we become His, and we have a growing relationship with God from that moment on."

Gene spread his hands to the sky and looked up, "Thank You, Father."

Sloan came over and spat in Gene's face. "Then why do you pray, old man?" As the brute asked the question, he dug a finger into one of the wounds on Gene's face. The cut began to bleed again.

Gene grimaced in pain and tried to lean away from the source of the pain, but Sloan just leaned in.

"I pray for you, I pray for me, I pray for my flock," Gene said.

Sloan's face, as Gene said, "I pray for you," went ashen, and he staggered back. His hands were still fresh with Gene's blood. He looked at his fingers and walked away. His face was dumbfounded, and he sought the other bucket of water that Benny had brought in. He shoved his hands in the water and began to scrub furiously at them.

Gene recognized a man who had just come face-to-face with the evil within him. *Oh, Father, let him see that You are the only way to get rid of those demons that reside within,* Gene prayed silently for Sloan.

Aaron now stood right in front of Gene. He looked down on him and motioned to Benny. "Tie his feet and hands to the chair, we don't want him flopping all around like a dying fish."

Benny's eyes were sad, and he walked over like a man who had a heavy weight on his back and bound Gene's feet and hands to the chair. The whole time Aaron was touching the electrodes of the cable together. The electrodes threw off sparks that banged and popped each time he brought them together. The man had an evil smile on his face each time and each time he brought the electrodes closer and closer to Gene's face.

After he did this ten or so times, he asked the question, "Well, Gene, where is your camp of believers at?"

Gene just shook his head.

Gene's world exploded in pain. He immediately tried to pull away from the fire that was making his muscles contract and his blood boil, but his binds held tight, and all he could do was jerk his body back and forth to get away from the pain. To Gene, it felt like the pain would never end. He could smell the hair on his arms burning, he could hear the crackle and pop of the electricity, and worse of all, he could hear his screams.

As quickly as it had started it ended, the burning was removed, and Gene's body slumped over in his captivity. His muscles spasmed and cramped as if he had been pushing a train for a mile.

As soon as he could think again, he prayed, "Lord, strengthen me and forgive them."

"Forgive them, forgive them, you can keep your forgiveness, old man. I just need the location of your camp so I can get paid."

The pain returned with a snap of electricity and a scream.

Gene lost all track of time. He measured the ticks of the clock by the application of electrodes. His world was condensed to the time when pain was being applied and when it was not. He did not know how long the shocks continued, but he finally heard whispered words that brought a sense of joy and relief.

"If you go any further, you are going to kill him," Benny said.

Gene heard the smack of a face being struck.

"You going soft on me, Benny?" Aaron asked.

"No, but if you kill him, our payday goes away. I want to get paid just as badly as you do. Let me tend to his wounds, give him food and drink. I can be nice, maybe that will loosen his tongue."

Gene could hear the hatred and contempt in Benny's voice, and if Gene was any judge of character, and he was, Aaron could hear it too. Gene fully expected Benny to be slapped again. Instead, he heard the electrodes drop to the floor.

Followed by, "Not a bad idea, Benny boy," Aaron said. "There may be hope for you yet, Sloan!" Aaron yelled.

"What?" Sloan shouted from across the warehouse.

"Put all of this away and clean up," Aaron barked his orders.

"Hey, that is Benny's job, not mine."

Gene heard Aaron growl. "Your job is whatever I tell you your job is your moron, now move."

Gene heard the shuffling feet of Sloan to fulfill Aaron's orders. He heard the far door slam as Aaron exited the warehouse. He had shut his eyes some time back and had been in prayer ever since the electrical shocks had begun. The Lord had allowed him to survive. He opened his eyes and examined his body. Burns covered his arms and chest. Right now, the electrical burns did not hurt as much as he thought they would have.

*Ah*, Gene thought, *I am in shock. Later he knows that the burns would be agony.*

"Lord, please deliver me from the hands of my torturers, but not my will but your will, Lord. I lift those that are doing this to me, forgive them, and lead them to you." As Gene prayed, he felt the bruises and cuts on his face close. He opened his eyes and saw the burns on his arms and chest turn from angry blistered burns to healthy skin. The only thing that did not return to normal was where his hair had been burned away those sections remained bald.

Gene heard a gasp of shock and looked up. Benny was standing there watching Gene's flesh heal. Benny could not move. All he could do was stare at Gene.

"You now see for yourself that God is real. You now see for yourself that He can heal those that follow Him. He can do much more than heal the flesh. Benny, He can heal your spirit, he can take away all the pain and hatred. He can restore you. All you must do is believe, and He will make you whole again."

Benny staggered back and dropped the rags he had been holding. "How…Wha…That is not possible," he stammered.

Gene just smiled and said, "It is not possible for man, but all things are possible through our Lord and Savior Jesus Christ. This puts you in a blessed position, Benny."

Benny turned away from Gene, trying very hard not to listen to him, but he engaged in conversation anyway.

"How does this make me blessed? I don't know what I just saw. You must possess some technology that heals you, or you are projecting the illusion that your wounds have been healed. All you people who believe as you do are liars. You fill people's heads with empty words and cheap tricks to fool the weak-minded."

Benny had worked himself into a frenzy. He spun back on Gene and punched right in the nose. Benny felt the nose break and blood spattered his fist and arm. He saw Gene's head snap back and saw the crooked nose.

Gene's head snapped back from the blow, and he grunted in pain. However, the pain was brief, and even as he brought his head back straight, his nose had healed. The only sign that he had been hit was the blood on his face.

Benny screamed, "I am not a weak-minded fool! Your tricks will not work on me, old man."

Gene shook his head slowly. "Oh, Benny, do you believe the lies so much that you cannot even believe what your own eyes are showing you? God has healed my wounds because He loves me, but more importantly, right now, He loves you, and He is showing you His love."

"This is trickery, that is all it is," Benny protested. "I know your cult uses tricks, and the media even say you use black magic to lure gullible people into your cult. I will not be fooled, old man. That is why the government is after you freaks, so the population will listen to reason and science and not some outdated fairy tales."

Gene gently and softly said, "Benny, look at me please."

Benny could not help but lift his head and look at the old man's face.

Benny saw an old man that he knew had been beaten and shocked. What he should see is a battered and burnt body, what he should see is loathing and hatred on the man's face, but instead, he saw, a man that did not have a mark on him. He saw a man that had joy on his face, a peaceful continence that shown bright like a beacon in the dark.

*How is this possible?* Benny thought.

"You mean to tell me that you think that the media and government are telling the truth? This is the same media and government that have been telling you that you must fear and hate. This is the same media and government that have imprisoned and killed people who dare to think for themselves. They force people to live in fear, so they have control over them. They convey a message of hate, so people will remain divided and not retaliate against them. The Bible says this about these times.

"Second Timothy 3:1–5 says, there will be terrible times in the last days. People will be lovers of themselves, lovers of money, boastful, proud, abusive, disobedient to their parents, ungrateful, unholy, without love, unforgiving, slanderous, without self-control, brutal, not lovers of good, treacherous, rash, conceited, lovers of pleasure rather than lovers of God-having a form of godliness but denying its power. Have nothing to do with them.

"Now compare that to what God is doing. God does not force anyone to follow Him. He offers everyone the choice of accepting His love or not. So ask yourself, Benny, which of these two, only offers slavery, and which one offers caring and love? Which one offers fear and hatred, and which one offers truth and salvation?"

Benny had no response he only turned and walked away. Gene heard the far door close gently, and he was alone once again.

"Lord, I pray that Benny will accept Your offer of salvation. Please open his eyes and let him see through the lies. In Jesus's name, I pray. Amen."

# CHAPTER 8

## *Mercy and Instruction*

The night passed agonizingly slowly. However, he had been a follower of Christ long enough to realize that God had a purpose for all of this. "Lord, while I understand that there is a reason for this, however, I still am a big enough wimp to complain about my captivity and the torture, if it is your will, please rescue me from this."

Gene's anxiety eased, and he fell asleep. He awoke and could not return to sleep. So finally, Gene decided to pass the time with a conversation with God.

"Dear Lord, why am I here? Please, Lord, deliver me from these evil men, but not my will but your will, dear Lord. You know, I say that, but do I really mean it, Lord? I mean there is no part of me that wants to stay here and be questioned and tortured. So how can I know if I really mean your will be done? I know that you can read my heart and my true intentions, but I have doubts. How can I truly know?"

Gene's body relaxed, he was at peace, and his mind before had been in turmoil and racing around like a cat searching for a hidden mouse. Now he was at peace, now he heard the Holy Spirit speak.

*Obedience* came the reply.

"Ah," Gene exhaled, "if I truly want your will to be done, then I will obey what you tell me to do, or in this case, I will stay where you tell me to stay." Gene sighed, and he knew that this was where God wanted him right now. He wanted nothing more than to be sitting around the campfire, telling stories to the children, but God wanted and needed him here. Hopefully, it was to protect his flock and to lead one or more of these people to God.

"Just to be absolutely clear, Lord, you are telling me to stay here?"

Gene laughed a moment later when no answer came. The answer had already been given. Gene laughed at his one last attempt to sway God into allowing him to leave.

For a few minutes, Gene rejoiced in his relationship with God. He remembered the young man that he had been, how reckless and angry. Always seeks to fill the empty place in his heart with human friendships, always choosing the wrong relationships to sacrifice himself for, always being betrayed and left. In his youth, Gene had a need to be accepted and liked by those around him. As a result, he had made some terrible choices of the people he hung around, basically anyone who would show him some attention.

Gene felt the familiar ping of pain as he remembered his old self, and then a peaceful smile leaped across his face as he remembered his salvation, maturation, and how the Lord had brought that about.

Gene had been raised in a Christian home. He had accepted Christ as his Savoir when he was thirteen years old. His childhood had been typical for a small-town boy. He went hunting and fishing, he camped out, he went to parties and football games, and he got drunk, just to look cool. Looking back on it, he had been very stupid. He went on to college, got a good job, and was looking to settle down, but that was not to be. Gene found himself among people who liked to party too much, and instead of influencing them to accept Christ, Gene out of his need to be accepted and liked by others allowed himself to be influenced into their way of life.

For ten years, Gene allowed himself to be led astray. Looking back, he realized that the Holy Spirit was trying to get his attention the entire time. When Gene had hit rock bottom, he shook his fist at heaven and screamed at God, "How could you do this to me?"

The reply from the Holy Spirit was calm, peaceful, loving, yet filled with authority. *"What makes you think I did this?"*

Gene fell to his knees and sobbed. He knew who had done this. "Lord, please forgive me. What can I do to make this right?"

*"Obey Me in just one thing I ask, and I will turn your life around in ways you cannot imagine."*

Gene, still with his face to the ground and sobbing, answered, "Yes, Lord, I will obey You, I will obey You all my days."

Since that time, Gene has been trying his best to obey God. Anytime he had not obeyed, he found that his life got messed up quickly, and he would seek God's will for his life again. God had kept His promise, and Gene's life had been amazing. He had witnessed, taught, mentored, led, and learned from his brothers and sisters in Christ. He had watched as people came to the kingdom of God. He had cried tears of joy with them and rejoiced as they grew in their relationship with God.

"Praise You, Father God, for You are worthy of praise."

The remembrance of the things Aaron and Sloan had done to him flashed into his mind. He wanted nothing more at that moment than to break out of this building, find them, and end their miserable lives. Then Gene began to justify these thoughts of vengeance.

"Lord, they seek not only to hurt me, but they seek to harm my flock. How can I just sit here and not try to protect those that mean so much to me?" Gene's cry was one of anguish and anger. The battle being waged within him was real. Gene got up and ran toward the door on the opposite side of the warehouse. He reached the door and hammered his fist against the cold steel. The bang of his fists echoed throughout the warehouse; it sounded like thunderclaps from a storm. The rage left him, and he slid to the floor.

As he sat there sobbing, a verse came unbidden into his mind. Vengeance is mine, says the Lord. Gene sobbed. "I know, Lord, but I am weak, and right now I hate them so much." Again, another verse came unbidden. *Blessed are the merciful for they will be shown mercy.*

Again, he heard the Holy Spirit speak, *Those that you call yours are Mine, and I will protect them.*

Gene hung his head, "Forgive my arrogance, Lord, forgive my selfishness. For I was not really thinking of my flock, only myself.

How can I do this, Lord? I don't have the strength for this. You are my God, you know I believe in you, but I am weak."

For the third time, Gene thought of a verse from God's holy word. *I can do all things in Christ who strengthens me.*

Gene understood fully now what God was asking of him. He was to stay here, he was to accept whatever came, and he was to forgive those doing these things to him. Not only did he have to forgive them, but also he had to try and witness to them the love of his Lord and Savior Jesus Christ. Gene understood that he would have to rely on God more than he ever had in the past to do all these things that the Lord was asking him to do.

Gene walked slowly back over to the chair he had been sitting in. As he walked, he said a prayer, "Lord, strengthen me so that I can do the things that Your will requires of me. Help me to not hate but to love, help me out of Your love to forgive those doing these things to me, and help me to be more like You, so I cannot only speak about You but show them You as well. Truly, Your will be done."

As he sat back down, he said, "In Jesus's holy name, I pray. Amen."

Just as Gene had finished his prayer, the steel door opened with a bang. Gene could not see the person's face from this distance, but judging by the size and shape, he knew it to be Sloan. Gene groaned, and out of the three he had to deal with so far, Sloan was the cruelest. He enjoyed making people suffer. He enjoyed seeing others in pain. Gene suspected that it was, so he did not think about his pain and suffering. The world can make you that way.

*What was the saying?* he thought, *Oh yes, better you than me. That is how Sloan lived his life.* It was better to see the other guy suffer than for him to be on the receiving end.

As the big man approached, he began slapping a thick piece of leather in his hand. The leather was about two feet in length. The smack of the leather and Sloan's demented grin filled the warehouse. Fear gripped Gene as he fully expected a resume of the torture. *Peace* came the gentle quiet voice, and Gene relaxed under the certainty of pain.

Sloan's grin became even wider as he saw the brief glimpse of fear cross Gene's face. Then Sloan frowned in dissatisfaction as he saw the calm overcome Gene. Sloan was close enough now, and he swung the leather, his frustration adding fuel to the blow. The strap came down across Gene's thighs, and he groaned in pain as his body flinched away from the burning in his thighs.

Sloan looked at Gene and smiled. He expected to see Gene crying, and while there were tears coming down his cheeks, his face was as serene as a windless lake. The strap came down again and again. The sound of a smacking pop filled the room. Each time the man flinched away from the pain and grunted, but he never tried to defend himself from the blow and always the face of tranquility returned.

"Agggh, what is it, old man? Do you enjoy pain? Is that it? Maybe this turns you on. What about it? Are you one of those freaks who enjoy getting pummeled? Why aren't you even trying to stop me from hitting you or trying to run away?"

Gene's gaze locked onto Sloan's brown eyes and said, "Fighting back is useless, and if I tried to run, I would be giving you exactly what you want. You see, Sloan, you want to see people afraid of you, you want to see them suffer, and you want to have power and control over people. That way, you think that people can't hurt you anymore. However, that kind of power is an illusion. Oh, you can hurt me all you want, but it will never be enough to fill that empty void in your heart. Only God can fill that void."

Sloan's eyes narrowed, his face turned red, and he shook with rage, but he did not swing the strap again.

Gene continued, "You see, only God can heal your heart, only God has the power to do that. When you seek to hurt people, you only succeed in doing further damage to yourself. Sloan allow God to heal you, ask Jesus to forgive you and live within your heart, and it will be healed. You will no longer have to hurt people to feel safe from them."

Sloan screamed at the top of his lungs as he brought the strap across Gene's face. "Shut up, shut up, shut up!"

Gene lost count of how many times he was hit in the head and face, but he felt every one of them. He would hate to look in a mirror right now, so it came as somewhat of a shock when the blow stopped. Gene could hear Sloan breathing hard and ragged, and he assumed that the only reason why the blows ceased was that Sloan was out of breath.

Through the ragged gasps, Sloan said, "I will kill you, old man, and you will know in the end who you should be afraid of."

Gene raised his head and, with a calm demeanor, spoke these words to Sloan, "In Luke 12:4–5, God's word says, 'I tell you, my friends, do not be afraid of those who kill the body and after that can do no more. But I will show you whom you should fear: Fear Him who, after the killing of the body, has power to throw you into hell.' Yes, I tell you, fear Him."

Sloan raised the strap to strike Gene again, but his arm fell back down at his side. Evidently, Gene thought he was tired, and Gene could not help but chuckle at God's irony.

Gene continued, "You see, Sloan, you surely do possess the power to kill me, but I do not fear you because you do not have the power to throw me into hell. I have made peace with the one who does, and I will spend my life in His kingdom when I leave this world. You, Sloan, have not. This should tell you where your fear should be directed. Make peace with God give your life to Jesus and be reconciled to God or spend eternity in hell, your choice."

With a scream of anger, Sloan began to beat Gene with the strap again, and at some point, Gene lost consciousness.

Gene awoke to the steel door banging closed. He opened one eye; the other was swollen shut again. His body felt like someone had beaten him. *Oh wait,* he thought they had. As the vision cleared in the one opened eye, he could just make out the shape of Benny. Was this Aaron's plan? To send them in here and torture him in shifts? How much time had passed since Sloan had used him as a human piñata?

"Lord, I am really ready to come home now because this sucks."

*Soon,* came the reply.

Benny was carrying bottled water and rags. He walked over and stood in front of Gene. He handed Gene the bottled water and said, "Drink."

Gene's hand shook as he took the bottle, opened it, and sipped at the water. His thirst demanded that he guzzle it, but Gene knew that was a bad idea. His stomach wasn't feeling up to large quantities of anything right now, and his lip was split in multiple locations, and easing water in caused less pain than downing the whole bottle.

Benny dabbed the rag in another bottle of water and began to gently tend to the cuts and bruises on Gene's face. "You are a fool. Aaron will get what he wants in the end. He always does, and if you don't tell him what he wants to know sooner rather than later, he will hand you over to Sloan, and Sloan will kill you. Just tell him where your people are. Save yourself."

Gene winced in pain at the initial touch of the rags, but while the cool water stung the cuts, they also soothed them a bit. He looked at Benny. "Do you consider it evil to betray those that you love?"

Benny had not expected a question and looked puzzled for a moment. "What?"

"Is it evil to betray the ones that you love?" Gene asked again. His voice was a little clearer now that the water had slid down his throat.

Benny's response was timid and unsure as if he was an animal inspecting a trap. "Well, sure, I guess."

Gene gave a little sigh and said, "Then I cannot give you or the one who sent you in here the information you want. I cannot speak evil, a good man does not speak evil, a good man brings things out of the good stored in his heart."

Benny's look was one of disbelief and confusion. "You think yourself to be a good man? Isn't that arrogant to think that? You think you are better than us?" Benny's last question was spat with anger and contempt.

Gene held up a hand and motioned for Benny to slow down. "Only because I have accepted Jesus as my Lord and Savior. I was just like you, Benny, lost and alone, wallowing in my sin and anguish. Then I made the decision to give my life to God, and since then,

He has made me a good man and put good things in my heart. The opposite of that is true as well. An evil man brings things out of the evil stored in his heart."

Benny's eyes darted around the large empty space as if he was being watched. Then he became suspicious again. "Oh yeah, how do you know that?"

Gene patted Benny's hand. "My boy, it is in God's word. It is in the Bible. Jesus told his disciples this to be true. It is in Luke 6:45, 'A good man brings things out of the good stored in his heart, and an evil man brings evil things out of the evil stored in his heart. For the mouth speaks what the heart is full of.' I do not speak anything that God has not taught me or given me to speak, hence I cannot speak evil, for I have God in my heart. Those that do not have God in their hearts have evil in their hearts and so they speak evil."

Benny stopped, wiping Gene's wounds, and slammed the rags to the floor. "You are trying to confuse me, old man." Benny's eyes were wide, and his breathing was as if he had been running a race.

Gene continued, "I am not trying to confuse you. I am trying to speak the truth to you. Your heart knows that I am speaking the truth, and the words I speak are in total contradiction to the lies that you have listened to and believed. They are directly opposed to the lies perpetrated by the world. This is the source of your confusion. This is the battle raging in you right now. It is a battle for your very soul."

Benny put his hands over his ears as if the words were causing physical pain, but Gene knew all too well that the pain ran much deeper than physical pain. Benny glared at Gene and ran to the steel door to escape the pain.

"Lord, draw close to Benny, help him to see and believe the truth," Gene whispered.

# CHAPTER 9

## *The Seductress*

There were no more visitors for the rest of the night, or at least what Gene assumed was the rest of the night. The wounds he sustained at Sloan's hands were screaming for attention. Sometimes the pain was bearable, other times not so much. At some point, Gene must have fallen asleep. Because when he heard the steel door open, he could see sunlight outside.

Gene had used the table as his bed, and he groggily rolled off it to stand on shaky legs. One of his eyes was still swollen shut, and the other was caked with sleep, so it was a little difficult to see the two people that were walking toward him. As they got closer, Gene could see that one was Aaron, but the other one was not one of Aaron's previous companions.

This one was a woman. She was dressed in skintight black pants with a tight black silk pullover shirt, and it had a picture of a dragon across her breast in silver and gold. She wore heavy makeup, but her face would have been much more beautiful if she did not wear so much. She was a very voluptuous black-haired beauty, who had learned long ago how to use her body and movements to get and keep men's attention. Although she was still young, the life she had lived was beginning to take its toll. Perhaps that is why she wears so much makeup now. The clack of her low heels rapped on the concrete floor, and she seemed to take pleasure in hearing the staccato of her walk.

As she drew closer Gene could see that she had an Asian ancestry, her eyes were a deep brown, slanted ever so slightly, and her nose was dainty and fit her heart-shaped face perfectly. Her lips were full and at the moment she held them in a pouty position. Gene could tell she was feigning annoyance with Aaron because while her face and lips said she was annoyed by all of this, her eyes were bright and shining at the pleasure of seeing a beaten old man.

Aaron and the woman stopped a few feet from where Gene was standing. Aaron pulled one of the chairs over and told Gene to sit. Gene complied because his legs were still shaky from the night of beatings.

The woman walked around Gene. Gene felt like a piece of prey that was being sized up by a dangerous predator. As she approached Aaron, she took a feigned step toward Gene and brought one of her heels down hard on the floor. The heel met the concrete floor and sounded like a gunshot going off. Gene was caught off guard by the step and flinched. The woman put her hand up to her mouth and giggled.

Aaron shook his finger at the woman and mockingly admonished her by saying, "Now, Mia, why do you want to frighten our guest so?"

He then draped an arm around her slender shoulders and leaned in for a kiss. She allowed the arm but did not allow him to kiss her. Instead, she gave him a playful punch in the stomach and said, "I'm bored. This is just an old man. You said that you had the key to all our dreams coming true. I thought you had finally scored enough money to get us out of this place, baby. Instead, you show me a broken-down shell of a man."

Mia turned her eyes toward Gene and, with an insincere smile, said in a voice that dripped with honey. "No offense."

Aaron disengaged his arm and stood to face her. She was only about five foot two inches tall, so the over six-foot Aaron had to lean down some to look her in the eye. "Mia, you don't understand. This man is the leader of the Christian cult that lives somewhere outside of the city. If we can get that location, the government will pay us a king's ransom for that information. He is a gold mine waiting to be tapped."

Mia smiled. "Really? Then why aren't we swimming in cash right this moment? I mean you have him here. What? Have you not even asked him the location of their camp yet?" The last was said with contempt, as if all men, especially Aaron, were buffoons.

Aaron's face became angry, and he yelled, "Of course, we have asked! This is a process that you would know nothing about. It takes time, but he will give up the location, I promise you that."

Mia became something different, then she sauntered up to Aaron and ran a hand slowly down his cheek and kissed him gently, yet seductively on his lips.

"Now, baby," she exhaled, "don't be angry with your Mia. Of course, I don't know anything about these things. I am just so anxious for you and me to be together forever in the lap of luxury as we deserve."

Aaron grabbed her, pulled her to him, and kissed her hard. She allowed this for a bit, but when she broke the embrace, she asked, "Can I stay and watch you get the information out of him? I have never seen a master such as yourself at work. It would be fun."

Aaron hesitated for a moment, "I don't know, Mia, you may not like what we have to do."

The pouty lips made their return. "Oh, baby, if it gets us what we want, I will enjoy every minute of it."

Aaron simply said, "Alright, stay here I will be back."

He quickly walked toward the door. Gene knew that the next torture session was coming, and with Mia here pushing Aaron, it would be worse than before.

Gene hung his head and prayed, "Oh, Lord, give me strength."

While his head was still down, he felt long slender, soft fingers caress his cheek. He looked up and looked into the eyes of evil. Mia stood there leaned very close to him and whispered. "You will give me what I want now, old man. He will do anything I ask. I could make things much more pleasant for you, even pleasurable. All I need is the location of your camp. Tell me now, while he is gone, and I promise you a night that will make you smile on your deathbed."

She leaned into Gene, her body rubbing up against him. Gene scooted the chair back and stared directly into her eyes. "Lady, I learned a long time ago if you consort with vipers, you get bit. No offense."

Her hand moved quickly, and she slapped Gene across his face. His head snapped back with the blow. He turned the other side of his face toward her and asked, "Would you care to slap the other side? It will not take away all of your pain and hate, but maybe you will feel a sense of accomplishment, as perverted and sick as that is."

Mia's face contorted in rage. Her true nature showed as she raked her long fingernails across Gene's closed eye.

Gene grunted in pain. He fell out of the chair and his feet pushed hard against the floor until his back was against the wall. He breathed heavily and brought his right hand up to his eye. Fresh blood ran down his face. As he opened his good eye, he saw Mia standing over him gloating, her fists clenched, and her hate-filled eyes burning into him.

"Hold out for a long time, old man!" she spat at him. "I am going to enjoy watching you suffer. You will give me what I want, and I get to see you break a piece at a time."

Gene smiled through the pain and said, "No, no, you won't, Mia. Stronger is He that is in me than he that is in the world."

"What does that even mean? Stronger is He that is in me than he that is in the world. Did they hit you in the head too hard? You're babbling nonsense."

Gene shook his head gently, his wounds were painful, and his heart was sad because he saw in all of these people lost souls. People who had been deceived by the evil in this world. People who really thought that they could save themselves were given enough time, money, power, or social media influence. The more they were fooled, the simpler the tool that they tried to use to save themselves.

"Look I have money, no one can harm me I am beyond the reach of God's judgment, or I am a social influencer on a device that millions of people look at daily, surely God won't judge me I am too important. I have power, and I can make people lose their jobs at a whim or kill them without a thought. God wouldn't dare harm me."

A tear rolled down Gene's face. "So many people are foolish enough to believe Satan's lies. So many people are destroyed by their own arrogance, pride, and lust for the lie of 'you don't need God, you are a god, and you can do whatever you want because there is no God, and there is no judgment.'"

When Gene's eyes met Mia's, she thought he wept for himself. "Ha, you are afraid, I knew it!"

She pranced around him and then started dancing, mocking him the whole time. "Where is your God now, old man? Why are you crying like a baby if your God is going to save you? Oh, we have won, and I am going to be rich when you break."

She stopped in front of him and planted a kiss on his lips and once again her body grinded on his. "Well, old man? Answer me!" she screamed.

Gene gently pushed her away and shook his head again in pity. Gene's voice was calm and peaceful as he responded.

"Oh, Mia, as with so many things, you have misunderstood my tears. My tears are not for myself, they are for all of you who do not know the love of my Savior, Jesus Christ. I do not weep because of what you will or will not do to me. I weep because I know what is going to happen to you if you do not accept the gift of salvation."

Mia's celebration tapered off, and she glared with hatred at Gene.

"You and Aaron think that I am here because you are clever or because of luck. I know I am here because this is where God wants me to be. I am here because at least one of you is still open to the message of good news, that God loves you and gave His only begotten Son for your salvation and redemption."

Mia looked as if she had been punched in the gut. Her dance of victory had become a sagging slump as she fell backward into the chair behind her. Her face contorted with rage, but she reacted like a puppet whose strings had been cut.

"Are you the one, Mia?" Gene reached out his hand to the young woman. "Are you the one whom God has sent me to give His message?"

Mia shrank back in fear now, her eyes were wide and locked onto Gene's hand. The hand that offered love and acceptance to her was a hot branding iron, and her feet backpedaled to push the chair further away from Gene.

Gene stood and took a step forward, his hand outstretched. "God has revealed to me the pain you have endured. The abusive parents, the string of lovers that used and abused you, your search for anything that would take the pain away. You have betrayed good people and hurt them before they could hurt you. You have stolen, betrayed, and even murdered, but even if you can be saved by Christ Jesus, all you must do is sincerely ask for His forgiveness and accept Him as Lord and Savior of your life. Please, Mia, God will heal your heart."

Mia's backpedaling stopped and a look of shock overtook her. She did not know this man, Gene, but he was telling her what she had done in her life. He knew things that she had never told anyone. Tears came unbidden to her eyes, and she cried.

"How do you…how could you know…" she stammered.

Gene smiled and said, "Because God's Holy Spirit lives in me. That is what is meant by greater is He that lives in me than he that lives in the world. The liar Satan lives in the world. When you are saved by Christ, God's holy spirit comes and lives in you. You are changed forever."

Mia took a tentative step forward and just then the steel door of the warehouse banged open, and Aaron's boots snapped on the concrete as he walked toward them.

The ray of hope that had been on Mia's face disappeared, and her rage and hatred returned.

"Oh wow, you are good, old man, you almost had me." She walked back up to Gene and spat in his face.

She spun and approached Aaron, "Get what we need my love and then please kill this old man for me. I can't stand the sight of him." She rubbed up against Aaron and gave him a passionate kiss and then all but ran from the warehouse.

Aaron had a puzzled look on his face but only for a moment. He then placed several rolled-up leather containers on the table and asked Gene, "Are you ready to talk old man?" As he unrolled the bags, gleaming sharp knives and pointed picks clanked.

The sight of the blades filled Gene with fear. He did not want to go through this, but he would not give up his brethren. Gene sighed and prayed, "Father, give me strength."

# CHAPTER 10

## *Ramping Up*

Aaron began by punching and beating Gene with a small baton. There were no questions, no conversation, there was just one blow after another. Gene finally collapsed to his knees from the beating. Gene was in good shape for a man of his age, but his muscles were bruised and battered. So when Aaron threw Gene on the wooden table face up and lashed him to it with heavy ropes, Gene could put up little resistance. Gene's arms were tied at the wrist and the ropes were tied to the bottom of the legs of the table. The same procedure was done to his ankles, and so Gene was spread eagle on a wooden table, and that is when he heard the scraping ting of a knife being sharpened on a whetstone.

Well, Gene thought at least he was sharpening the knives before cutting into me. Gene knew from experience that the cut of a dull knife hurt worse and took longer to heal. It was at that moment that Gene was amazed by his line of thought. *Really? Sharp knife cuts versus dull knife cuts, this is where his mind was?*

Not surprising really, he had grown up in the countryside, learning to hunt and fish, so he knew about keeping knives sharp. This was how he knew also that Aaron was sharpening the knives and not dulling them. He could tell by the ringing sound of the metal being drawn across the stone.

Then Aaron stood above him. He had a nine-inch clip-point blade in his hands. The handle was made of some type of hardwood.

Gene could not tell what type as Aaron gripped the knife tightly in his right hand. From what Gene could see, Aaron had done a nice job sharpening the blade as its edge flickered and gleamed in the light of the warehouse.

"Well, Gene, are you ready to talk to me about the whereabouts of your camp?"

Gene was about to tell him no once again, but God's holy spirit reminded Gene that there was a way that he would tell Aaron the location of the camp. If Aaron accepted Christ as his Savior, then Gene would reveal the location, Torture while horrifying to Gene was not going to pry the answers Aaron wanted out of Gene. The holy spirit of God would see to that, so Aaron's and Gene's only hope at this point was to witness to this man who was about to torture him. *Wow, Lord, you really do call your servants to some bizarre situations.*

"Given our current circumstances, the answer would have to be no," Gene replied.

"Are you sure you want to say no? I mean, what is about to happen here is very unpleasant. You could stop all of this, and all you have to do is tell me where your base is," Aaron countered. His offer seemed to be genuine. Was there a part of him that did not want to torture an old man?

"Aaron, the only way that I would ever tell you what you want to know, is if you were a believer in Christ. So instead of torturing me allow me to tell you about my Lord and Savior. He saved me, and He can save you. He loves you and is waiting for you to accept His sal—"

Gene's words were cut off in a grunt and growl of pain as the blade Aaron was holding began to slice deeply into his forearm. *Father,* Gene silently prayed, *give me strength. In Jesus's name. I pray.*

A second cut two inches from the first. The cuts were three inches in length and were designed to inflict pain, not bleed the person out. Aaron was very careful not to cut too deep. It was also very important not to hit any major arteries or veins. A dead man does not give up information.

His mentor, a man Aaron had later killed, would be so proud of the precision of Aaron's cuts. Unlike Sloan who just pounded on people until he either killed them or they gave in, Aaron considered himself an artist at inflicting pain. The key to gathering the information was to inflict pain. Let the person feel that pain for a while and then be sympathetic. You had to convince the person that you did not want to continue, and they had the power to make it stop.

What Aaron found incredible was that even though Gene knew he was about to be tortured, he still was trying to talk about this Jesus.

*These guys are really insane*, Aaron thought as he made the third cut on Gene's forearm.

It had taken four cuts to get around Gene's forearms. The man's arms were muscular from a lifetime of work, Aaron guessed. Gene struggled, moaned, and grunted in pain each time the knife did its work. Aaron put the knife down after the last cut and reached for a bandage on the roll-around cart that he had brought in. The bandage was so Gene didn't bleed more than necessary, but beyond that, it was not a kindness. Aaron wrapped the bandage around Gene's injured arm, and Gene's scream echoed through the warehouse. The bandage was laced with salt and lemon juice.

Gene had known pain during his lifetime, but nothing had prepared him for this. The cuts were painful, and he sighed with relief when Aaron laid the knife aside. Gene had tears running down his cheeks and was amazed to see Aaron about to bandage his arm. Gene could smell the lemon juice, and he had seen the grains of salt. He thought, *This is going to hurt*. Then his world exploded in a searing burn as the bandage was applied. Gene could not stop the scream that escaped his lips.

After Gene's screams subsided into growls of pain, Aaron explained as if he was teaching a class, "You see it is not enough to simply make the cuts. You must make sure that the initial pain of the cuts stays with your subject for a while. Hence the salt and lemon juice. Effective, yes, now let's get started on the other arm."

Gene glared at Aaron; his eyes gleamed with hatred. Now this was what Aaron expected; this was the first sign that his plan would be successful. Then just as Aaron saw the hatred, he saw the man's face become serene, and the anguished hatred look vanished from his features. Then he heard something he had never heard his subjects say.

Gene had a moment where all he wanted was to get out these ropes and strangle the life out of Aaron, then the holy spirit of God spoke to him and reminded Gene that He loved Aaron as well, and Gene was not here to kill the man, he was here to save him.

Even as Aaron repeated the procedure on his other arm, Gene prayed, "Lord Jesus, forgive me and forgive Aaron. Please lead him to You. Please love him as You have loved me."

Aaron was dumbfounded for a moment and then recovered as he said to Gene, "Old man, if you think playing that game will gain you sympathy from me, you are dead wrong. I am looking to get paid here, and you are nothing but the key to that treasure."

Despite the pain he was in, Gene smiled. God was at work in others even when they did not believe. "Funny you should use the word *treasure*." Gene grunted as a sharp wave of pain rolled up both arms. Gene continued after the wave of pain's initial fire slowed into an ember, "You see, the treasure you seek is of this world and will be gone faster than you think. The treasure God seeks to give is the treasure that God offers you through His Son, Jesus Christ. His treasure is eternal and never fades or rusts. He can give you the kingdom of heaven. The treasure you seek is earthly, you must commit evil acts to obtain it, and it will be taken from you by one that has betrayed others before. Please, Aaron, listen to what I am telling you. God loves you and would save you from the damnation that is coming your way."

Aaron paused his work on the wrappings for Gene's other arm which he had just finished cutting. The whole while this man did not flinch. He just kept talking about his salvation, that he was trying to save him. This was a first for Aaron. In his time of getting information out of people, he had been cursed, he had been threatened, he had been swung on, and even one guy had broken his bounds and tried to strangle him with his bare hands. But he had never had someone try to save him from damnation. Initially, Aaron just silently laughed at the old fool, finding his behavior ludicrous. Now he found this man's behavior disturbing. This man was supposed to hate him at this point, not confessing his love for him and certainly not this God's love he kept talking about.

Aaron finished wrapping the lemon salt cloths on Gene's wounds. The man would not shut up about God. Aaron could feel his temper rising as Gene spoke. This was an odd sensation for Aaron. Why should he be angry? He was not being tortured.

Aaron heard Gene say, "In the name of Jesus our Lord…" Aaron's hand shot out with the speed and strength of youth, slapped Gene across the face, and then grabbed him around the neck. He slammed Gene's head back against the table.

"Shut up, old man! Shut up, shut up, shut up!" he screamed. With each shut up, his hand tightened its grip on Gene's throat. "I do not know what your game is, but I promise you, you are only making this worse for yourself."

"We will see how willing you are to speak when you deal with the burning pain for a few hours." Aaron removed his hands from Gene. What was wrong with him? Aaron realized that he had never been this angry with one that he had tortured. He was the one who was supposed to be in control here, and yet, he had lost his temper. This turned out to be the weirdest interrogation of his life.

"Ah, Aaron," Gene slurred hoarsely. "You are more afraid than I am. The weirdness and disturbing feelings you are having are from doubt and fear. Somewhere deep inside of you, you know my words to be true. God loves you and seeks your salvation."

Aaron raised his hand to slap the old man again. Upon seeing the look of tranquility on his face, Aaron all but ran from the warehouse.

A thought hit him as he slid the heavy steel doors aside and exited the warehouse. In every other interrogation, Aaron always felt in control.

*Why do I feel that the old man is the one in control?* The thought made Aaron's blood run cold.

"O Lord," Gene whispered his prayer, "I see you working, and I thank You for it. If it is Your will, can You speed up the process? It is awfully uncomfortable here." Gene's soft chuckle filled the empty warehouse.

*Soon* came the response, and Gene laid his head down on the table and passed out.

Gene became vaguely aware of someone turning his head back and forth. He slowly came out of the black of unconsciousness. As he did, he realized that someone was not turning his head. They were slapping him, evidently trying to wake him up. His eyes popped open at about the same time his ears started working again. He saw Mia over him slapping his face over and over.

"Wake up, please wake up." Mia's violence ceased as soon as she saw Gene's eyes open. The ravaging beast once again became the purring kitten. "I am so sorry, but I just had to get you to wake up. Are you okay? Here let me get you some water."

Mia slinked over to a bottle of water and came back and put Gene's lips to the bottle. Gene sipped at the water gratefully. When Mia saw that he was done, she put the lid back on the water and sat it back on the end of the roller cart. Mia came back and hovered over Gene. She lifted his head as much as the ropes would allow, and she placed Gene's face into her ample bosom.

"Thank you, Gene, I have seen the light and have accepted Jesus as my Savior. You were so right. He has saved me from everything I have ever done wrong in my life. How can I ever repay you?"

A muffled reply was all that Mia heard.

"What?" she asked as she pulled Gene's head back.

Gene breathed in a quick breath and said, "I said you could take my face out of your breast so I can breathe."

Mia gave a little schoolgirl laugh and said, "I am sorry I am just so happy now that I am saved."

"You're saved?" Gene asked.

"Yes, isn't it wonderful?"

"Why yes, that is wonderful." Gene looked at Mia and wondered. *Lord*, he thought, *is this woman before me truly saved? Allow me to see through Your eyes, Lord. Allow me to see if she is now my sister in Christ.*

"I will get you out of here. I have places I can hide you until they give up looking for you. Then we can be together."

Gene's face locked in surprise and disbelief. "We? Together? What do you mean by that, Mia?"

"When I spoke with Jesus and asked for forgiveness, He told me that I was to be with you. I am to be your reward for all the years you have helped people."

Gene began to laugh. His arms hurt, his head hurt, and his throat hurt, but he could not help the guffaw of laughter that started from his toes and worked its way all up his body.

Mia was confused at first but began laughing as well. She reached for Gene again to hug him, but Gene pulled his head away as much as he could. Mia stopped but continued to laugh with Gene.

Once both stopped laughing, Mia spoke, "I am so excited for this new life of ours to begin. I cannot wait to meet all our friends. I'm nervous. Will they like me? Will they approve of me? Oh, what am I saying? Here I am worrying about that, and you're still tied down to a table suffering. I will cut you loose, we will escape this place, and then our lives can begin."

With a deft flick of her wrist, a blade appeared out of Mia's sleeve, and she began to cut at Gene's bounds. After only a few minutes Gene's limbs were free and he sat up slowly. As feeling returned to where the ropes had been, pinpricks of tingling and pain from where the rope had cut into his flesh reminded him of just how much straining he had been doing against his imprisonment and torture.

"Hurry let's get out of here," Mia said. She offered a slender hand to assist Gene in getting off the table.

As she grabbed his arm, Gene stiffened in pain. The squeeze of pressure had sent a fresh wave of the concoction that covered his arms shooting into his wounds, and the pain almost made him fall off the table.

Mia kept pulling and trying to get him to stand. Gene placed a hand on hers and asked, "Please give me a moment, Mia."

Mia let go of his arm and said, "I'm so sorry. I'm afraid of being caught. You have no idea what Aaron will do to me if he finds me helping you to escape. Besides that, I am anxious to begin our lives together. We will be so happy together."

Mia smiled at Gene. Her smile was beautiful and had led many men astray. Mia was accustomed to getting what she wanted out of men without much effort. Gene had been reading her and listening carefully to her words, now he knew, the Holy Spirit had been speaking to him through these observations of her.

"Mia, you say that God has told you that you are to be mine. That we are to be together?"

"Yes," she said. Her soft tender hands reached out and stroked his cheek. "I so look forward to our lives together, but we can talk about that another time. We must get out of here first. We must get to safety."

Gene chuckled.

Mia shot him a look, one that belied her previous concern and compassion. "Why do you laugh?"

Gene sighed and said, "Mia, God does not work that way. All of this is a lie. It is your pitiful attempt to get me to reveal to you where my brothers and sisters are. It will not work."

Mia sobbed. "No, I promise I prayed, and God has saved me." She put her hands over her face and began to cry.

"Alright," Gene said. "If this is so, then you will not mind if we examine it."

"What!" Mia exclaimed as she spread her arms out wide. She paced around the table like a cat in a cage. "You have got to be kidding me. We do not have time for this. We must go now." The last word was said with desperation and anger.

Gene waved his hand at her in a *wait* gesture. "May I tell you a couple of ways that Christians recognize other Christians?"

Gene saw that Mia was getting more agitated by the minute. She breathed out a heavy sigh, and in a voice that was more recognizable as the person he had first met, she said, "If you must."

Gene held up his injured right hand and lifted his index finger slowly. "The first way is what is called Fruits of the Spirit. These are, according to Galatians 5:22–23, 'The fruit of the Spirit is love, joy, peace, patience, kindness, goodness, gentleness, and self-control.'" Gene held up the second finger on his right and continued. "The second one according to the word of God is found in John 13:34–35.

Jesus told his disciples, 'A new command I give to you: Love one another. As I have loved you, so you must love one another. As I have loved you, so you must love one another. By this, all men will know that you are my disciples if you love one another.'"

Mia looked dumbfounded. "Gene, we must leave. We do not have time for you to quote whatever this is to me. I am scared, please." She shook him, trying to get him to get up and come with her.

Gene just stayed seated. "I know. You are scared that Aaron will discover that you are trying to betray him. You are scared that I have discovered your lie. However, you're mainly scared that what I have been telling you is true. I have seen through your ruse that you do not exhibit the fruits of the Spirit. You do not show any love for me or anyone else. You are still exhibiting selfishness, lack of control, and impatience. These are not fruits of the Spirit. You still only love yourself. Therefore, I do not recognize you as a disciple of Christ. Your only concern right now is that we leave so that you do not have to share the wealth that, you think, will come if you discover the location of our camp. Finally, you insist that we will be together. The problem with that is that God knows I have only loved one woman, and that is my wife, and God would never do anything to break that bond."

Mia's face turned from sweet innocence to one of rage as she brought both of her fists down into the middle of Gene's crouch. Gene doubled over in a fetal position. No sound came out of his mouth as he had no breath to utter any sound. His whole body was now paralyzed with excruciating pain.

Mia got down right in his face. Spit flew out of her mouth and hit Gene in the face as she screamed, "You stupid fool, my way you at least could have had some pleasure, some fun! Now I will leave you to Aaron's way, which is nothing but pain and suffering."

She raked her perfectly manicured claws across his face. Gene could only make out her silhouette as she neared the doors; however, there was no mistaking the angry crack of her heels as she left the building.

# CHAPTER 11

## *The Next Treatment*

Gene saw Aaron enter the building. The man was rubbing his cheek and laughing. Gene could see the red mark on Aaron's cheek, and the man was still smiling. The smile was sadistic and had a hint of pleasure to it.

Aaron saw the quizzical look on Gene's face and simply said, "Women," as he chuckled and shook his head.

Gene readjusted himself in his restraints, trying without success to find a more comfortable position. He looked at Aaron and said, "I take it that Mia was not happy to see you."

Aaron's face flashed brief anger, and then the smile returned. "Mia is only happy when she is getting what she wants. I think I have you to thank for the slap I just got. What did you do to piss her off so bad?"

Gene shrugged and instantly regretted it. The battering and the cuts made any movement painful. Through a moan of pain, Gene said, "I rejected her advances and called her out when she tried to convince me she was now a Christian. If it is any consolation to you, she used her fingernails on me, while you only got a slap."

He saw the gashes on Gene's face, they had to be painful, yet the man still had a sense of humor about it. Aaron's look he gave Gene was one of amazement, and there was genuine amusement as he said, "Humor, you still have a sense of humor amid all of this? I will say this for you, you are one resilient old man. This is going to be more of a challenge than I thought."

Gene shook his head and quietly spoke. "Whatever strength or resiliency, as you put it, I have is from God not from myself. I am not a tough old man. I am a Christian man in the midst of persecution and torture. My God is here, and he is waiting on you, Aaron."

"Well, Gene, if he is waiting on me then it is going to be a long wait."

Without hesitation, Gene spoke, "God is patient, and He has all the time in the world, but you do not, my friend. The time of God's judgment is at hand. You do not want to find yourself on the wrong side of that judgment. It is time that you allowed God to speak to your heart. It is time that you let go of the abusive father you had. It is time that you stop blaming your mistakes on others and come to realize that you are the one who has made bad choices that have led you to be the person that you are now. The fact that you had a father that ignored you, and then a stepfather that beat you, will not be enough. It is not an excuse that your friends put the guns and knives in your hands at such an early age, you are still the one who used those guns and knives to inflict harm and pain. Each of us is held accountable for the decisions that we make. Each one of us will be held accountable for the sins that we commit, regardless of who or what began the process. Every person will stand before Jesus in the end, and whether it was my dad's fault, or it was my friend's fault will not be a defense. There is only one way that you can be forgiven and redeemed to God the Father, and that is His son Jesus Christ."

Aaron had unsheathed a knife from a holster on his hip. He had brought it up to begin cutting away the lemon salt-soaked bandages and his hand froze in midair. His mind was stunned for a moment. How could this man that he had never met, know these things about him? He had never once spoken of his childhood to anyone.

Aaron's gaze was one of astonishment as he looked into the kind blue eyes of his victim. Then his false bravado reappeared. "I see my reputation proceeds me," he said as he puffed out his chest a little. "I must be more famous than even I realize if you have that many specifics on me."

Gene's smile was one of compassion and pity. "No, Aaron, before today, I had never heard of you. God has revealed to me your sufferings and your pain. God is reaching out to you. He seeks to save you, to have a relationship with you, because He loves you. The reason I am here is to convey God's love to you. The reason I am here is to bring you the good news of salvation. It is not too late, all that is needed to be saved is to believe that Jesus died for your sins and took your place on the cross. Confess your sins to God and ask for forgiveness in the name of our Lord and Savior Jesus Christ."

Aaron turned his back and began to pace like a captured animal in a zoo. After a few minutes of this, he stopped, whirled back on Gene, and spat, "You think that spouting this nonsense is going to stop me from getting the information that I want? Do you think that saying these things is going to save you? I could just kill you right now. Here, let me show you how powerful your God is."

Aaron walked quickly toward Gene and, in a fit of rage, brought the knife crashing down toward Gene's chest. Just before the knife struck home, Aaron's hand stopped, and try as he might, he could not plunge the knife into Gene's heart.

Gene whispered a prayer, "Thank You, Lord, for saving my life. Thank You for sparing Aaron the guilt of another life taken, in Jesus's name. Amen. My life is not yours to take, my life belongs to the Lord of all creation. It is God and only God that determines when my life on this earth is to end."

Aaron continued to try and dive the knife into Gene's chest and after several more attempts, he slumped over in exhaustion. Breathing hard, as if he had been pushing a truck up a hill, he glared at Gene. "How are you doing that?"

Gene smiled. "You are the one that wanted to prove how powerful my God is. He just showed you how powerful He is. As I said, I am not doing any of this. Jesus Christ, my Lord and Savior, still has work for me to do. It is not my time yet. Right now, my work is to witness to you, Aaron. Which is good news indeed because it means that there is still hope for you, Aaron Krauss, son of Don Krauss."

Aaron staggered back and screamed, "How do you know that, old man? That is impossible."

For the first time in years, Aaron felt he was not in control. This could not be happening. This had to be a trick. Aaron flung the knife aside and went over to Gene, he searched Gene for any kind of communication equipment, thinking the old man was bugged and someone was passing information to him to rattle him. Aaron found nothing.

Gene just lay there as he was being searched, and once Aaron was satisfied that he did not have any bugs on him, he said, "I spoke the truth. God's holy spirit is where and how I know what I know. Dear God, please show Aaron more of Your power and glory, in Jesus's name. Amen."

Aaron walked over and picked up his knife. As he got to the table, he began to cut off the bandages. "If your God is protecting you, how is it that He has allowed me to hurt you and cause you pain? Once I reapply your treatment, I am going to start on your legs, so buckle in, Gene, it is time for the next treatment."

Aaron began removing the bandages from Gene's arms. As he was doing so, Gene let out a sigh of relief. Aaron had never heard of or seen this reaction before. He quickened his pace, virtually tearing off the bandages now, and what he saw when they were removed shook him to his core.

His voice shaking and hands trembling, Aaron whispered, "How's that possible?" The knife hung limp in Aaron's right hand and what was left of the bandages clung to his fingernails. His knees felt weak as if they had turned to jelly, and he could not take his eyes off the healed flesh of his victim. "You should be in agony. What did you do? How did you do this?"

It was not possible. Gene's arms should have been in massive cuts, swelling, and blistering, with an angry red tint to them. The man should have been screaming as the bandages had been removed. Instead, what Aaron was looking at was pink healthy skin, not a blemish on either one, and not only was there no screaming, but Gene's face also was at peace, and his voice had a calm demeanor to it as Aaron heard him speak.

Gene turned his eyes toward heaven and, in a reverent voice, said, "Praise You, God, thank You, Father. I did nothing, Aaron, but

God did. You asked why God allowed you to hurt me. It was so you could see God's power and glory with your own eyes. Touch the flesh, Aaron, and see that it is whole once more. This is not for my sake. Although I am grateful, this is for your sake."

"No!" Aaron screamed and slashed across Gene's left arm with the knife. He felt the knife rip through flesh, saw blood spurt from Gene's body, and heard Gene scream as the pain racked him.

Gene's scream of pain became a moan of contentment as his arm was healed once again.

Aaron's breath came in great heaves as he experienced the adrenaline rush of inflicting pain, as he felt the control, he so desperately needed return. Then just as quickly as he experienced this, he saw the wound on Gene's arm close. It knitted itself completely, and there was no trace that any harm had ever been done.

Tears ran down Gene's face, and he once again prayed, "Thank You, Lord Jesus, once again, You reach out to this man and show him Your glory, thank You." Gene then raised his eyes toward Aaron. "God does not normally show His miracles this overtly, at least not these days. He must have a very special mission for you, my brother."

Aaron's eyes were wide with terror, and his lips quivered. It took several moments before he responded to Gene. "I am not your brother. I am your torturer. You will give me what I want, or I will kill you." Aaron's face was a mask of desperation. He looked around as if he was expecting a bolt of lightning to hit him or a door to open so he could escape.

Gene could not tell which one Aaron was hoping for more.

Aaron once again tried to bring the knife down to kill Gene, and once again, he could not get the knife to plunge home. Just another eight inches and he could be free of this old man's nonsense, he thought. However, despite all his efforts, he could not end the old man's life. In exasperation, Aaron flung the knife to the ground. The clanking tinging sound of metal meeting concrete sounded like peels of thunder in Aaron's head. He took one last look at Gene and fled out the double doors of the warehouse.

Just before the door slid shut with a clang, Gene heard Aaron say, "How is this possible?"

Gene smiled, lifted his eyes toward heaven, and simply said, "God, my brother, God is how this is possible." Gene heard Aaron scream, "What! How? Shut up."

"Wow, Lord, You really are pulling out all the stops on this one. He must be more stubborn than I was, thank You, Lord."

# CHAPTER 12

## I Will Save You

Jonathan had been in the sewers underneath the warehouse for hours. He knew he would never get the stench out of his clothes, and to make matters worse, he had worn his favorite shoes. Jonathan allowed himself a chuckle at the ridiculous thoughts running through his mind. Here he was at least thirty feet underground, listening to his mentor, friend, and brother in Christ being tortured, and his mind goes to how his clothes will be ruined.

What silly things the mind will think about when under stress. Jonathan felt helpless, he had heard Uncle Gene being tortured, he had heard his screams of pain, he had heard him deny the temptress, and he now heard him witnessing to the one known as Aaron.

He had wanted to run to the camp and mount a rescue party for Uncle Gene as soon as he had discovered where he was. However, God's holy spirit had told him to stay where he was and to listen. Jonathan had always had a good memory, but now he remembered everything. He remembered every sound, word, smell, and sight that he beheld. God had supercharged his senses. Jonathan knew enough to realize that God wanted him to remember every part of this night, and he could not help but wonder why.

*No*, came the scream from above. Jonathan knew that was Aaron. Then he heard Uncle Gene scream, but that scream was cut off by a moaning sigh of relief. He could feel panic coming from above him. At first, he thought it was Uncle Gene, but it was not, it was Uncle Gene's torturer. It was the one called Aaron.

He could hear Uncle Gene witnessing to Aaron, he heard Aaron threaten to kill Uncle Gene, and Jonathan's heart caught in his throat as he heard someone straining. He could envision Aaron trying to plunge the knife into Uncle Gene's heart. Tears rolled down Jonathan's face, and he turned to run. He had to get to Uncle Gene. He had to stop this madman from killing his brother. Jonathan only moved one step, and his body froze in place.

A peace filled Jonathan, and the voice that he heard was one of pure joy, calm, and serene in every aspect.

*Gene is mine to protect. Stay.*

Jonathan turned his attention back to the unfolding drama above his head. Jonathan heard metal bouncing hard off the concrete. He heard Aaron say, "How is this possible?" He heard heavy footsteps as if someone was running away. He heard the heavy clang of a metal door being slammed shut.

He heard Uncle Gene's exclamation of wow and heard him praising the Lord, then there was silence.

Jonathan listened for some time. He heard nothing coming from above. He prayed, "Lord Jesus, please let me get my brother out of there, but not my will but Yours, oh, Lord." Jonathan was at peace, and he shouldn't be. His brother in Christ was being brutalized, and he was being prevented from helping. "Why, Lord, why are You doing this?"

Jonathan had been a follower of Christ long enough to know the calm, peaceful voice of the Holy Spirit. So when his answer came, he knew where it was from. In his heart and head, he heard. "You question, why didn't you just pray my will be done? Then with the next breath, you question God's will. It seems that you want my will to be done if it fits with what you want."

Jonathan had been chastised like this before. God was still teaching him, shaping him, and sometimes the lessons were painful to learn.

Jonathan bowed his head. "I am sorry, Lord, please forgive me, in Jesus's name." As soon as he submitted himself to the will of God, Jonathan heard, *Speak to My servant Gene. He will hear you.*

"Thank You, Lord," Jonathan said.

"Uncle Gene, it is Jonathan. I am below you in the sewers. What can I do? How can I help you?" The last question was said in a broken sobbing voice. Every fiber of Jonathan's being screamed for him to act, for him to rescue Uncle Gene.

"Jonathan? Oh, thank God that you are all right. What are you doing here boy? Get out of here. You must not be caught. Leave here at once."

Following Uncle Gene's commands was ingrained in Jonathan now, and he turned to go but stopped. "No, Uncle Gene, God has me here for a reason. He told me to find you. I have been here for hours. I do not know exactly why I am here, but I think God wants me to hear all of this. I am struggling though. I want to rescue you. I want to pull you out of there and away from these horrible people. God has prevented that. All I can do right now is stay and listen."

Gene smiled. "Trust in the Lord's understanding, my boy. He will reveal to you why you are here and what you are to do in time. I take comfort that you are here with me."

"Why is God doing this, Uncle Gene?"

Gene took a deep breath and let it out slowly. "There is at least one lost soul here that can be saved. God has called me to witness that lost soul. I believe it is the one called Aaron. You heard our last exchange?"

"Yes, I did. What freaked him out so that he ran from the warehouse?"

Gene chuckled. Jonathan had heard that tone in Gene's laughter before. It was the one he used when God showed up and did something unexpected and often miraculous.

"God healed the wounds that Aaron had inflicted upon me right before his eyes. Aaron's reaction was one of a crazed animal, and he attempted to kill me. God stopped him. For perhaps the first time in that young man's life, he witnessed the power of God, and of course, it freaked him out. For the first time, he is being forced to contemplate the existence of God and, therefore, his ill-spent life. The mirror of salvation has been placed right in front of him, and he does not like what he sees."

"Ouch," Jonathan exclaimed. "I remember how painful that was. So you believe that God is breaking Aaron's heart so that he can heal it?"

"Yes, my boy, I do," Gene said. "I also think there are others here that can be saved. Therefore, God has me here."

Jonathan knew that they were to witness whenever and however they could to those who were lost, but he loved Uncle Gene and all he wanted to do was get him out of there. "But, Uncle Gene, they could kill you. We both know that just because we witness someone does not mean that they will accept the gift of salvation. Please let me go get our brothers. Let me get you out of there before it is too late."

Uncle Gene's voice took on the tone of command. "Boy, I am here at God's will. You will do nothing that is against that will. If God calls me home, then He calls me home. I will die filled with His peace and joy knowing that I was about His work, and if I die, I will be with Him in glory. Heed my words. Do what God instructs you to do, nothing more, nothing less. Do I make myself clear, Jonathan?"

Jonathan was transported back to when he was a teenager. He had heard that commanding tone before, and he knew that it was not to be challenged.

"Yes, sir," Jonathan responded. "God had told him what he needed to do. He should've listened to God, but God knew, of course, that he had to hear it from Uncle Gene." Jonathan sobbed, and then he prayed. "Lord, forgive my stubbornness, help me to listen, trust, and obey. Lord, please give my brother, Gene, all that he needs to fulfill the mission that you have for him. Help us, oh Lord, to walk in your light. Help us to deny ourselves. Help us to be closer to you with each passing minute of each day, in Jesus's name, I pray."

"Amen and thank you, Jonathan. Jonathan, I do not want to die. I want to survive this and go home and teach the children again, but that is up to the Lord. We must put our trust in God, not man.

"I understand, Uncle," Jonathan replied. "I want to do God's will, but I am still confused as to whether I should stay here or go and get help. I could stay here and record the history witnessing to these people."

At that moment, a flash of blinding light split the darkness, so bright that Jonathan could see it down in the sewers. A split second later, a boom of thunder was so loud that Jonathan covered his ears.

"Wow, that was loud."

Gene spoke in a mild confident tone. "That was God getting your attention. He has been speaking to you, but you continue to doubt, so He used His outside voice."

Jonathan blushed, shook his head, and then said, "So you think God wants me to leave now."

This time the lighting was a gentle strobe across the sky and the thunder a musical rumble. Gene simply said, "I believe you have your answer, my boy."

Jonathan bowed his head and replied, "Yes, Lord, I will obey."

Gene laughed, a sharing, loving laugh, as he said, "Remember what Psalms 19:1 says, my boy. The heavens declare the glory of God; the skies proclaim the work of His hands. God has shown His glory, God has spoken to you. Go from here and follow God the rest of your days, Jonathan, know that God loves you and I love you."

Jonathan's eyes filled with tears. His heart was heavy with sorrow and yet filled with joy. He may never get to see Uncle Gene again. His voice broke as he said, "I love you, sir, thank you for all you have done for me. I can never repay you. I don't want to leave, I know I must, but it is like ripping a piece of me away. Please, Lord, let me stay."

The night sky once again was split open with the white-hot light of lighting, and the peal of thunder was even louder.

"There is your answer, boy, go. Do not worry. I will see you again."

Nothing more was said. Jonathan took step after agonizing step at first, and as he obeyed God's will, his steps became easier. He still was struggling with leaving Uncle Gene behind, but he knew he was doing God's will, and his heart was at peace. He knew God would take care of Uncle Gene much better than he could ever hope to.

God had told him, *Gene's well-being is not in doubt.*

Jonathan shook his head in disgust as he darted between the rubble-strewn streets. To himself, he muttered, "How does God put up with all my doubt and second-guessing? You would think I would've learned by now."

*Love and you are learning*, came the reply.

Jonathan smiled, and his pace quickened as his heart became lighter with the joy of the Lord.

# CHAPTER 13

## Broken Heart

Aaron slammed the warehouse door and, for the first few steps, ran away from the man inside. Then he realized that if his gang saw him rattled, they would not hesitate to take him out, especially Sloan. He forced himself to walk at a normal pace. He slowed his breathing down and took on his normal, cross-me-and-die attitude. However, he knew that nothing was normal. What had just happened? What had he seen? Thinking about it caused him to start hyperventilating again.

*No*, he thought, *just get to your room. Don't think about it until you get to your room.*

*Wait*, he thought, *the guards are at the door. No...* He had dismissed them hours ago. They had not seen his weakness.

Aaron took a deep settling breath and realized that the sun was rising behind the building he was headed toward. The shadows of the long night were giving way to light. The building he headed to was another smaller warehouse. This one had an upstairs office in it that served as his quarters. The rest of his group had bunks downstairs. It was good enough for them. It had been a long night, he needed sleep, but before sleep, for some reason, he wanted—he needed—to see this sunrise.

Aaron walked around the building and looked to the east. The sun was just peaking above the horizon. The flair of light set the sky bursting with color. Purples, oranges, pinks, and blues lined the clouds in the sky. The black of the night gave way to the blue skies and golden rays of light from the big furnace in the sky. Aaron gazed in wonder. "I don't think I have ever looked at a sunrise," he said aloud. "It is beautiful." Then Aaron heard Gene's voice in his head. *Remember what Psalms 19:1 says, my boy.* "The heavens declare the glory of God; the skies proclaim the work of His hands."

A tear ran down Aaron's cheek, and once he felt the tickle of the drop on his skin, he angrily rubbed it away. "What is wrong with you? Some charlatan pulls a trick, and you fall to pieces. You start to believe in God. Is that it? Do you believe in God now, Aaron?"

His voice was angry, bordering on manic. He could not show weakness like this, His crew, and the people he did business with were jackals, they would strike at the first sign that he was going soft.

"Bah, I just need sleep." Aaron walked back around the smaller warehouse, opened the sliding door, and went inside. *When I wake, no more Mister Nice Guy with that old man. I will break him and get paid. Money and power are the only things that work in this world, and I intend to get mine*, he thought.

Walking through the warehouse, he saw twenty or so of his people sitting around, some together, others by themselves. Cots and makeshift beds lined the floors. The windows at the top of the building had been broken so the smoke from the fires could be released. Two or three of the fires burned, probably cooking whatever they had for breakfast.

Some of his followers sat around talking, some were still drinking from the night before. He smelled urine and vomit coming from the back side of the building. As he looked around, he could not understand how or why he was there. The fact that he was surrounded by the unwashed human dregs of society really made him angry. The anger swelled inside of him until it burst forth.

"Hey!" he screamed. "Clean this pig stye up. It stinks in here. Do something useful or leave."

For a moment, everyone just stared at him. Then some began to laugh, they thought he was joking. One of the most offensive laughs came from a fat man who was relieving himself in one of the corners. With a flick of his hand and wrist, Aaron drew a knife and threw it.

The blade sank deep into the back of the man's left leg. The howl of pain echoed through the building, and all of a sudden, everyone began cleaning. They had no idea what had brought this on, but when Aaron was throwing knives at people, they didn't ask questions, they just obeyed.

Aaron didn't show it but, that throw of the knife had shaken him. He had been aiming for the fat slob's head. That was the first time he had missed a throw in five years. The knife had been meant to kill, but it had only caused injury. *What had just happened? What is going on with me?* Aaron mused. Then he remembered he needed to sleep, and he told himself that was the reason he missed. He knew it was a lie.

Feeling even more troubled now than before, Aaron ascended the stairs to his office/bedroom. He hoped that he could sleep. He should be able to after all; he had shown them once again who was boss. They did not see weakness. They saw strength, they saw someone who could end them if they did not obey. This was control; this was power. He could now sleep without worry of being killed in his sleep, of course, the fact that he locked his door and slept with knives under his pillow also assured a peaceful slumber.

Aaron sat on the bed and pulled off his shoes and socks. He lay down on his back with his left arm across his eyes. He drew a deep breath and began to drift off to sleep. As he did, he remembered the words he had heard Gene say, "Remember what Psalms 19:1 says, my boy. The heavens declare the glory of God; the skies proclaim the work of His hands." He thought about the beauty of the sunrise he had just seen. This was his final thought as sleep took him.

Aaron's stomach grumbled, he could stand to eat, but the thought of eating also made him nauseated. No, what he needed now was sleep. Aaron laid down. His body was ridged with tension, and he could not get out of his mind what had just happened with Gene. He had never seen anything like it. He had not imagined it. He had seen with his own eyes, Gene's wounds heal. One moment there was cut flesh and dried blood, then there was healthy skin. How? Why? He had never heard of anyone or anything that had been able to heal wounds like he had just seen.

*It had to be a trick*, he thought. Maybe Gene had drugged him in some way? No, that didn't make sense, Gene had been under his control ever since he had been brought in. Try as he might, Aaron could not make sense of what he had witnessed. Gene claimed it was God. He even prayed and thanked God for healing him. If there was a God, then that part at least made sense. If God had healed Gene, then it stands to reason that Gene would thank him for it.

What didn't make any sense to Aaron was that Gene prayed more for me than he did for himself. Why would Gene do that? Aaron had brutalized him, tortured him, and wanted information from him that would lead to his friends' arrest and probable death. If anything, Gene should be praying for God to strike him down, or at the very least for escape.

Aaron rubbed his eyes. His head hurt and swam from the torrid thoughts bouncing around in his head. He needed sleep but he didn't think it would come, but he would close his eyes just for a few minutes; if for no other reason than to try and calm his nerves.

Aaron sat straight up in bed. His body was covered in sweat, and he was shivering. Light poured in from the windows. He rubbed at his face and thought, *Man, I didn't sleep long*. Then he realized that the light pouring into the room was not coming from outside. It came from an old chest that he kept his personal belongings in, it contained all the things that were important to him. They were few, but no one better has messed with them.

Aaron's head whipped left and right. Who had come in here? He knew he had locked the door. How did they get in? However, as he looked no one was in the room except him and the light from the chest got brighter.

Aaron rolled out of bed and walked over to the chest. He took out a key and unlocked it. "I am going to kill whoever did this. I am in no mood to be pranked." Aaron reached out with his right hand and flung the chest open.

A golden blinding light leapt from the chest and Aaron screamed in pain as the light burned him. He could not see, he rubbed both arms they were not blistered, but the light hurt, and it seared him.

Visions of the world he lived in filled his mind.

Aaron saw every camp around the world that held the radical terrorist threat known as Christians. Camps, what a wonderful euphonism. These were prisons. Concentration camps like the ones he had seen in black market historical videos. He saw the squalor that they were forced to live in. He saw every atrocity known to man being perpetrated on them. He saw them being beaten, tortured, raped, and killed. He saw the ones that were doing all these things laughing and placing bets on how long the victim would last.

As all these visions ran through his mind, he saw the Christian terrorist praying for those doing the torture. One man was being burned inch by inch with a torch, the skin blistering and peeling away. His screams were real, but each time his tortures paused he prayed for them. Aaron heard his prayer.

"Father, I know You love all of us, please forgive these men and women. They have been deceived. Father, show them your mercy, show them Your love. Save them, Father, before it is too late, in Jesus's name I pray. Amen."

Then the torture would begin again, and the screams would begin again.

Another man had his head placed in a guillotine. The man with his hand on the lever to bring down the blade asked, "You have been found guilty of sedition and terrorism against the state. The sentence is death. Do you have any last words?"

The man did not fight or show any signs of fear. His face was peaceful as he said, "Father forgive th—" His prayer was literally cut off as the guillotine blade came down with a sickening sliding noise of the descending blade and the man's head separating from his body.

"Guess not," the man with his hand on the lever laughed.

Aaron was transported to a home where a mother, father, and two children gathered around a table in their living room. The father was reading from the Bible. The front door exploded inward and troops in black body armor and helmets poured into the house. As they entered the room where the family was, their weapons trained on them. The father rose in surprise and placed his body between the man and his family.

"Please no," the father pleaded. "We have done nothing wrong."

The man in charge walked into the room and looked at the table where the father had laid the Bible. An explosion boomed and fire shot from the end of the pistol, and just that quick the mother and children had watched their husband and father executed in front of their eyes.

Aaron awoke screaming. His hands were out in front of his face in a defensive position. He rolled and fell out of his cot and hit the floor with a thud. It was only then that he realized that he was not dead. He had been the father a few seconds ago.

Aaron lay there on the cold concrete floor of his room curled up in a ball and sobbed. His heart was broken for all he had seen, all he had done. It was at this moment that Aaron realized that he had also been the people committing the atrocities in his visions. He could not move; all he could do was lay there and cry.

After several minutes of mind-numbing guilt and debilitating sobbing, Aaron stood up and walked over to the mirror on the wall. He saw his face, but when he looked into his eyes, he discovered that he hated the person staring back at him. Why? This made no sense. "I am who I am. I have never felt remorse for who I am or what I must do to survive. What the hell is happening to me?"

Only a few seconds had passed since Aaron had looked into the mirror, but it seemed he had been standing there for hours. Finally, he lowered his gaze and saw the basin of water on the table below the mirror.

"Okay, time to snap out of it." Aaron cupped his hands and dipped them into the water. The water was cool, and Aaron took it and splashed it over his face several times. He took a towel from the table and dried his face off.

"There, that's better, feeling more like myself now. It is time to get back to work. It is time I got this drivel out of my head. It is time to break that old man and get paid."

As Aaron straightened up, he saw his face in the mirror again. Except this time, it was the covered face of the man who had shot the father in his dream. Aaron staggered backward. He instinctively reached for a knife and flicked it at the man in the mirror. The blade struck true right between the eyes of the man in the mirror. Only when Aaron looked again, the face with the knife protruding from it was his face.

His legs trembled, his hands shook, and he knew he must be going crazy. He walked over unlocked the door and descended the stairs in a haze of mental anguish and confusion.

# CHAPTER 14

## The Report

The figure in the shadows watched as Aaron walked down the stairs from his room. He had heard crying and cursing coming from the room of his so-called leader. This was the moment he had been waiting for, Aaron had never shown a chink in his armor, and he had never shown a weakness before. He had now, and as the informant climbed down the rope he had installed, he knew this was his moment, and this was when he took control.

All he had to do was make his way to the authorities and report. Aaron was showing signs of sympathy for the old man. Christians like the old man deserved no sympathy, they deserved to be put down like the leches on society they were. After all, mankind had been held accountable for their moral standards long enough. Everyone knew that there was no God, and it had been just a story that those in power told everyone else to keep them buried under the chains of those who had money. From now on, he would be the one who had the money, and he would be the one who had power.

He had learned this in school, he had learned it from the government he now served. Christians sought to divide and exclude people from their club, and everyone knew that inclusion and serving the greater good of the government's agenda was the way to make the world a better place. As he walked out of the warehouse on his way to inform Aaron and the Christian scum, he just knew he was about to make the world a better place, especially for him.

He took a circuitous route through the garbage-strewn streets known as the warehouse district. He was always very careful not to be followed. It just would not do if any of the gang knew what he was doing. Most of them were loyal to Aaron because he kept food in their bellies and a roof over their heads. He had once thought as they did until he realized he should be the leader of the gang. Why shouldn't he be the one in charge? It was at that point; he knew if he just kept his eyes and ears open that Aaron would one day slip up and he would cash in on the big man's mistake.

His route took him into a section of the city that used to be famous for its high-end shops and restaurants. The streets were not as filthy here, but the fall of the city was still very much in evidence. There were not many snobby shops or restaurants left, but a few still survived.

The night was chilly and damp, but it was normal for Autumn. A few streetlamps still worked here so you only got a glimpse of the overcast sky. Nighttime was not a safe time to be out and about, but he had no worries. He was armed and if provoked very dangerous.

Making this trip was always a pain, but his contact refused to come down to the docks. He always wanted to meet in this one restaurant; if memory served him, it used to be called John Dino's. At one point it was a high-class Italian joint, now it served some edible spaghetti, and if the owner could bribe the right officials, some veal.

He stopped just across the street from his destination. He took one more look around to make sure he had not been followed and then proceeded to cross the street and enter Dino's. The bell above the door chimed softly, alerting the staff that a new customer had arrived. The hostess looked up and gave him a half-hearted smile.

"How many in your party, sir?" she asked as she came around the podium.

She was dressed in what once had been a slinky black evening gown. Now it was torn, and threadbare, but she still struck a handsome figure in the dress.

He held his hand to stop her and said, "I am meeting someone here. I'm sure I can find him."

She stopped, turned, and went back to standing behind the podium. All semblance of civility and willingness to help evaporated as she turned away.

He walked to the back of the restaurant and found a man sitting there slurping up what passed for spaghetti. He wore a brown suit jacket, brown pants, and a white button-down shirt with a pink tie, and his tan overcoat was draped across the back of his seat.

He had the look of a long-time bureaucrat. His hair at one time brown was now streaked with gray and thinning on the top. His plump face had grown even more gaunt and strained since their last encounter. He was around six feet tall and had a not-too-plump belly. What gave people the creeps when they looked at him was his eyes. They were gray and squinty, and they had the look of a predator. The eyes screamed show no sign of weakness, or I would pounce.

He looked up just long enough from slurping pasta to say, "Well, what ya got for me?"

"Nice to see you too, Rogan. May I sit down?"

The man nodded and pointed at a chair with his fork. Bits of sauce and a strand of pasta plopped onto the red checkered tablecloth as he did.

Sloan could not stand the pariah he sat down next to, let alone, sit here, and eat a meal with him. Sloan just kept telling himself that the jerk was a means to an end. A way to get to his goal, so he pushed down his disgust and tried his best to be friendly.

"What is good here?" he asked.

Rogan Blass looked up and glared at his companion. "Cut the crap, Sloan. What do ya got for me?"

Sloan took a menu from the table and studied it for a moment before waving a waiter over and placing his order for a plate of pasta. He ordered red wine to wash it down with. This last order got Rogan's attention. His fork stopped halfway to his mouth, and then he put it down completely.

"You spring for your own drink. You must have something juicy."

Sloan's smile was all teeth, as he took a breadstick and chomped down heavily on it. "What I got is going to get your career back on track, and it is going to make me a rich and powerful man."

Rogan glared at him. "You mean it's going to make us rich and powerful men, and that's only if I think the information is worth it."

The two men just stared for several moments. Sloan continued to devour his breadstick, while Rogan had completely forgotten his plate of spaghetti.

"Okay enough of this alpha-dog crap," Rogan said. "You best remember who you're talking to Sloan. I am the one with the official job with the government. You are just an informant. One word from me and you are under a jail cell for a long time. After all, I'm the one with real power here. I tolerate you and your people because I need information about the Christian scum. All I need do is snap my fingers and you are done."

A twinge of guilt pinged through Sloan. He couldn't believe he was about to sell Aaron to this skag of a human. Then it passed, and Sloan remembered his goal of being rich and powerful. If selling out Aaron or any number of his friends meant he would live his life out in luxury, so be it.

"What I have is a leader of the Christian community named Uncle Gene. What I have is Aaron torturing this Gene fellow for information about his cult's whereabouts, and instead of getting the information from this guy, Aaron is listening to this Gene's Jesus message, and it is starting to mess with his head. I think he is going soft. I think he is going to allow this guy to escape. I think you need to bring both in for questioning, and of course, I will expect my just reward for bringing in Christians and the collaborators. That is what I have, Rogan."

The waiter who had taken Sloan's order came back and placed Sloan's spaghetti plate in front of him, he held a parmesan grinder out asking if Sloan would want some more cheese on his pasta.

Sloan glanced up, nodded his head once, and the young man turned the handle of the grinder. Cheese dropped over the red sauce, and it was hot enough to melt the cheese into the sauce. The smell of the food made Sloan's mouth water, he had not been hungry when he had come in, but now he was ravenous.

Sloan held up his hand and the waiter stopped the grinding. He then placed a glass in front of Sloan and poured a deep red liquid from the bottle he had pulled off the cart behind him.

As the waiter pulled the bottle off the cart, just for a second, Sloan could not see what was in the young man's hand. Sloan tensed and reached to the middle of his back, where he carried a very illegal handgun. He was able to identify the bottle before he pulled the gun, but he was sure that Rogan had seen his reaction. That was not good.

"Thank you," Sloan said as the waiter finished and left the table.

Sloan dug into his food as if nothing had happened. Perhaps Rogan had not seen his flinch.

Rogan leaned back in his chair and wiped his mouth with his napkin. The predator's smile and the gleam in his eyes told Sloan all he needed to know.

"My…my we are jumpy tonight," Rogan said as he leaned forward and locked his beady eyes onto Sloan. "I really hope for the sake of our friendship that you don't have a gun on you. You know only government employees are allowed the right to be armed. The second amendment doesn't exist anymore."

Sloan never looked up from his dinner and continued to shovel food into his mouth as he said. "Na, I know better than that, why would I change it? After all, I'm about to be a rich man."

Rogan picked up a toothpick off the table and began to pick his teeth. He knew Sloan was lying, but he did need the information and Sloan was right it would make them both wealthy and powerful. Rogan didn't think Sloan even knew the bounty on this Uncle Gene. The last Rogan had heard was Ten-Million World Credits. That was enough to allow a person to live the rest of their lives in filthy luxury. So for right now, Rogan could overlook Sloan's transgression until, of course, it came time to split the loot. He could always tell the police to arrest Sloan on a charge and throw away the key, or if it came down to it, kill Sloan. After all, who would miss him?

The staff of the restaurant was beginning to close the place down for the night. Rogan slipped a twenty-credit note on the table and got up to leave.

"Dinners on me, my friend. Leave a message in our drop point twenty-four hours before you want us to move in, and soon after that, we both can quit our day jobs. Well, I can, do you have a job, Sloan? I mean other than being a low life that is."

Sloan glared at Rogan. "Thanks for the meal and Rogan."

Rogan turned back to look at Sloan.

"We are both lowlifes. You just work for a corrupt system that takes betrayal to a whole new level. Besides, from what I have seen, being a low life pays off big."

Rogan put his overcoat on and said as he walked away, "You know, Sloan, you are smarter than you put on. That's a good thing for us lowlifes."

Sloan smiled as he stuffed the last of the spaghetti down his throat. "Indeed."

Sloan thought about taking the twenty and running out the door, but he might have to come back here at some point. So instead he left it and walked back out into the cold damp night. *Not long now*, he thought, *not long now*, as he disappeared into the shadows.

# CHAPTER 15

## Jesus Is the Way

Gene had dozed on and off throughout the day. It was now late afternoon. He could see the sun setting through the windows near the roof of his prison. As he woke this time, his mind drifted to Jonathan. Surely, he had returned to the cave by now. A momentary wave of sadness swept through him. Part of him wanted Jonathan to come back and rescue him. Part of him wanted to see Jonathan's face, to hear his voice once more. Gene knew though that their paths lay in different directions now. They were both about their Father's business and doing God's will was the most important thing.

*Besides,* Gene thought, *I will see him again either in this life or in heaven.*

Gene was still tied to the table. It was uncomfortable, but at least God had healed his wounds. Gene closed his eyes and prayed.

"Father, I miss my flock. I miss the comforts of my home. I confess to you that I would rather be there than here. Please forgive my weakness and strengthen me for what is to come. Lord, I can see you working on Aaron. I see the pain in his spirit. I see the turmoil that radiates off him like the sunlight bouncing off a still lake. Father, give me the words to reach this young man. Your will be done, Lord. In Jesus's name, I pray. Amen."

Just as Gene finished his prayer, the steel doors at the end of the warehouse grated and then opened. Gene could see Aaron striding toward him. His stride was angry and confident. Gene dreaded an arrogant and angry Aaron, for it meant that he was back to do his worst to get Gene to reveal the location of the cave.

As Aaron drew closer though Gene saw that the young man's seemingly confident gate was impeded by trembling legs and Gene also noticed that Aaron's hands shook ever so slightly. As Aaron drew closer, Gene could clearly see the signs of a rough night. Aaron's eyes were sagging, and he had a haunted fearful look that Gene knew all too well. God had been speaking and teaching Aaron during the night. Gene's heart leaped. There was still hope for this young man. God was working on him. God was showing him his sin. God was breaking his heart so it could be healed.

"How did you sleep?" Gene asked.

Aaron stopped dead in his tracks only a few steps from the table where Gene lay tied up.

"What...what do you mean by that, old man?" Aaron snapped the question back like an animal that was trapped.

Gene smiled. "I simply mean, how did you sleep? It has been my experience that when God has something to say to someone, they normally do not get a good night's sleep. So once again how did you sleep, Aaron?"

Aaron closed the distance between them like a cat pouncing on its prey. The knife was in his hand and at Gene's throat in a heartbeat. In a growling animalistic voice, Aaron spat, "What have you done to me, old man? Tell me now or I swear that I will kill you right here, right now."

Gene's face was peaceful as he answered his assailant. "I have done nothing, my young captor. What you are experiencing is God trying to get your attention. God is showing you the sin that you and the rest of this world are living in. This is good news for you, Aaron. God is trying to save you. He loves you and wants to have a personal relationship with you."

The knife came away from Gene's throat. Despite his willingness to die for God's kingdom, Gene breathed a sigh of relief.

Aaron took a step back and put away the knife. Gene could see that he was still angry, and it was evident when the next questions snapped from Aaron's lips.

"What is your part in this old man? Why do you care what happens to me?"

Gene smiled again and his face was filled with joy as he answered.

"Oh, Aaron, I am simply the messenger. God has blessed me to be the one who carries his message of love and salvation to you. As to why I care, I care because this is what Jesus has taught his disciples. Love one another. He gave us the great commission to go out unto all the world and spread the good news of His salvation. In the Bible, in Mark 16:16–17, Jesus gives us this command, 'Go into all the world and preach the good news to all creation. Whoever believes and is baptized will be saved, but whoever does not believe will be condemned.' I am simply fulfilling my Lord's command."

Aaron stood there looking at Gene as if looking at a crazy person. He could not believe what he was hearing. "You know I can kill you at any time. You are willing to die to carry out this great commission. You know that is crazy."

Gene chuckled. "I can see why you and the world think so, but it is not insanity, dear boy. It is love."

Gene saw the look of disbelief on Aaron's face. Gene shifted his weight on the table and took a deep breath. *Okay, Lord, here we go. Open his eyes, Lord*, Gene thought.

"All fall short of receiving God's love and mercy. Everyone in this world is sinful. All are disobedient to God. Jesus gave His life so that all who believed in Him would be forgiven and be reconciled to God the Father. Jesus gave His life so that all who believed in Him would not perish but have eternal life. The only way to bridge the gap between the sinful world and God is Jesus's sacrifice and resurrection."

Gene looked at Aaron for any kind of reaction. What he saw on Aaron's face was pain and confusion. *Well, Lord, so far, a normal reaction to your good news*, Gene thought and then continued, "The Bible tells us, For God so loved the world that he gave His only begotten son that whosoever shall believe in Him shall not perish but have eternal life." This is in John 3:16. The Bible also tells us that there is no greater love than this, that he lay down his life for his fellow man. This is in John 15:13. So you say that I am crazy, you say that me being willing to lay down my life is crazy. God says there is no greater love than this. You think I am crazy because of what the world considers sane? Look at the world, Aaron. It is hateful, spiteful, sinful, deceitful, and people willingly sell their fellow man out for a loaf of bread. So, Aaron, who would you say is sane and who is crazy? I follow Jesus who has already given His life for all mankind out of love. You follow a world that would just as soon stab you in the back and not care where your body falls. So who is the crazy one here, Aaron?"

Anger flashed in Aaron's eyes as Gene challenged his perceptions of sanity, but only for a moment. Gene could see that Aaron was thoughtful after his initial reaction.

Then Gene saw Aaron's jaw set, and Aaron spoke, "So you're telling me that you follow a dead man? You really are an idiot. I have no time for idiots. Tell me where your base is, and you may live through this." Aaron slowly slid one of his blades from its sheath; the threat was not lost on Gene.

Gene's face was at peace in the face of the blade. The look on Aaron's face was one of shock.

*Why isn't this old man scared?* Aaron's mind screamed at him.

"Jesus did die. In fact, he was tortured worse than anyone ever has been, then he was crucified on a cross. One of the worst ways to die. However, death could not hold him. He is the Son of God. On the third day, He arose, and He was resurrected. He is in heaven now with God the Father, and one day He will return to claim those who believe in Him, and they will live with Him in heaven forever. No, Aaron, I do not follow a dead man. I follow the Son of the living God. To answer your second question—no."

Aaron leaned in close to Gene, his blade coming inches from the old man's blue eyes. "So you say this Jesus rose from the dead. How could you possibly know that? You are just telling lies, old man, to try and save your butt. It won't work. Now spill!" Aaron screamed at Gene.

Aaron had brought the knife's cutting edge toward Gene's cheek. Gene could feel the pressure of it increasing. This was Aaron's ploy to get him to spill as he had put it. Gene was scared, but the

Holy Spirit kept his heart rate even, his breathing steady, and his face calm as he spoke.

"How do I know? I know because Jesus walked among His followers for forty days after he escaped the grave. I know because over 1,200 people saw Him, spoke with Him, and heard Him preach. This is not mythology. These are facts recorded by eyewitnesses to these events, and they are recorded in the Bible. Lastly, I know because the Bible, the holy word of God tells us, and the word of God is truth."

Aaron flicked the blade, and Gene winced as Aaron put a small cut just below his right eye. Aaron stepped back from Gene and said in a low threatening tone.

"I don't believe any of this. All of this is you just trying to distract me. You are so full of it. How do you expect anyone to believe this drivel? Everyone knows there is no God."

Aaron paced back and forth now, getting more agitated with each step.

Gene smiled a knowing smile and said, "If this is such drivel, as you so eloquently put it. Why are you so curious? Why do you continue to ask questions about my Jesus? Why are you so upset by what I am saying? If you truly do not believe, then none of what I am saying should bother you, none of what I am saying should elicit questions from you. What you are experiencing, Aaron, is God trying to reach you. You are fighting by falling back on lies that you have been told, by trying to rationalize your way out of believing. You can't, you have been witnessed to, and now you have a choice to make. Either accept the gift of salvation from Jesus and have eternal life with Him in heaven or reject His gift and spend eternity in hell."

Aaron's head snapped around, and he glared at the bound old man on the table. "Did you just threaten me, old man?" Aaron walked slowly toward Gene.

"No," Gene replied calmly. "I simply told you the reward and consequences of the upcoming decision you must make."

Aaron stopped, turned, and headed back to the double doors. He put the knife away slowly, put his hands to his face, and screamed. After the gut-wrenching scream, he stopped and turned back toward Gene, and with tears rolling down his face, he said, "You do not know what I have done. If you did, you would not even be speaking to me. Let alone trying to save me."

Gene shook his head. "Oh, Aaron, God knows what you have done, and He loves you still. Why do you think He has me here, witnessing to you? We all fall short of the mercy and grace of God. That's why Jesus sacrificed Himself so we did not have to earn the Father's forgiveness, but it had already been purchased through the blood of our Savior, Christ Jesus."

Aaron turned and walked all the way to the double doors of the warehouse. Once there, he stared at the hasp of the locking mechanism for several minutes. He took a padlock out of his pockets and slid the bar of the lock through the hasp. The loud click of the padlock seemed to have a finality about it; as if, there was no turning back from this moment.

Aaron walked back over to Gene. He untied him, set him up, got him some water, and placed him gently in a chair.

"Tell me more," Aaron said as he sat down across the table from Gene.

Gene rubbed his wrist and tried to get some feeling back in his feet by flexing his ankles back and forth. *Thank You, Lord*, Gene thought as he responded to Aaron.

"Well, you see, my friend, Jesus is the way."

# CHAPTER 16

## *Gene the Sinner*

"Perhaps this will be easier to explain to you if I tell you my testimony. You see God didn't just save me once but twice. The truth is that God works on us from the time we are saved to have a closer relationship with Him."

Aaron's face clouded in confusion.

Gene nodded his head and smiled. "Listen to my story, my friend, and all will be revealed."

Aaron could not believe his ears, this man whom he had tortured was calling him his friend. No one was that stupid. Surely this old man knew by now that Aaron was his enemy, not his friend. This must be a ploy, a trick to gain my confidence, a ruse to make me let my guard down.

Gene laughed, and some of the water he had been drinking spewed out the side of his mouth. He wiped his mouth with his sleeve and said, "This is not a trick or ruse. This is the truth."

Aaron's mouth dropped open in surprise. "How the hell do you do that, old man? Can you read minds?"

Gene just shook his head. "No, the spiritual gift that I have received from the Holy Spirit is an ability to read people, and sometimes that Spirit of the Most High reveals more than mere nonverbal observation can reveal."

Aaron looked suspicious. "I have to tell you, old man, it is unnerving, freaky, and downright scary."

Gene winked at Aaron and smiled. "To tell you the truth, there are times it scares me as well, but enough about that, let me tell you my story."

Gene took another sip of water, set the bottle down on the table, took a deep breath, and began his testimony.

"You see, Aaron, I was most fortunate because I was born into a Christian household. From the start, I was taught about God, His Son, Jesus Christ, and the holy spirit of God. I was taught about His endless love, mercy, grace, power, and eternalness of His nature. So it was no surprise that at the age of thirteen, I accepted Jesus as my Lord and Savior. I was forgiven of my sins, I was changed, and I no longer wanted to do the sinful things of my past. For a time, I walked with God, and God walked with me. My relationship with God grew."

Aaron seized on this thinking that he had caught Gene in a lie. "I thought you said God never abandons those who believe in Him. You just said that he did abandon you when you said for a time."

Gene closed his eyes, and a tear trickled down his face as he remembered.

"Oh, Aaron, God never did and never will abandon me. However, there was a time in my life when I abandoned Him. You see, in my youth, my twenties, to be precise, I wanted to be important. I wanted to have friends and be in the center of things. My need for acceptance from those around me led me to make decisions that were not based on God's will but on my own. Consequently, instead of witnessing to others about Christ, I allowed myself to be swayed into a life of sin, a life devoid of the joy of God, a life that is condoned by this world. I was still saved, but I was living my life in sin, just so I could impress the wrong people, just so I could be accepted by people that professed friendship but had no idea what the word truly means."

Aaron pointed his finger at Gene. "Wait, if God had saved you, how could He allow you to sin? How could He say He loves you and allow you to make those mistakes still?"

"My friend, God does not make or want slaves of us. He wants a relationship with us. Even those of us who have been saved can make stupid mistakes. We still have free will, and we can choose to go down a path that God never wanted us to go down. I chose the path I went on; it was a wrong path and it led me to be in places I never should have been and do things I never should have done."

"Why didn't God bring you off this path then?" Aaron shot the questions out there with anger. He was determined to find a flaw in Gene's story about God.

"He did over a ten-year period. God tried to get my attention and correct me back onto the path He had for me, but I continually refused. I ignored all of God's attempts to rectify my mistakes. For ten years, God tried to lovingly and gently bring me back to where I was supposed to be—in a relationship with Him, but, alas, in my youth, I was stubborn, and on some level, I thought I did not need God anymore."

Gene sighed, bowed his head, and said, "Thank You, Father, for never giving up on me. Thank You for Your chastisement, thank You for loving me enough to continuously reach out, and thank You for the final blow that brought me back to Your loving arms."

Aaron picked up the final blow part. His interest was really peaked now. "Final blow, what final blow? Did God strike you? What happened?"

Gene could not help himself. "Are you sure you want to hear the rest? After all, this is a story about God's love. I thought you said there is no God."

Anger flashed across Aaron's face. "Bah, tell the story, old man, or would you rather I resume torturing you?"

Gene held up his hand and smiled. "No, forgive me, I have a quirky sense of humor and couldn't resist making you squirm a bit."

Aaron's hands flicked and a knife appeared in each. He pointed both at Gene. "No more jokes, old man. I see no reason for humor, and neither should you. You have not convinced me of anything yet."

Gene sighed again and nodded his head. "I will continue. Please put away your toys."

Aaron rankled at his knives being called toys, but he put them away just the same. His face had anger in it still, but it was being replaced by curiosity. The fact that the man in front of him was telling him about his sinful past and being so open about his guilt was unheard of today. No one took responsibility for their actions anymore. Everyone knew that it was always someone else's fault, or at the very least, it was just the way things were. There was no guilt or justice; there was simply survival. The fact that Gene made himself the villain of the story intrigued Aaron.

Gene rubbed his hands, even after all these years he still felt the sting of what happened. He remembered all too well the crushing blow of guilt and shame, and while he was eternally grateful to God for that blow, he still wished it had never been necessary. He looked Aaron straight in the eyes and continued.

"You see, God had continued to bless me even though I was not obeying Him. I was making more money than was good for someone of my age. However, instead of using this wealth to help others or be a good steward of what God had blessed me with, I used it to party and basically buy friends. If I had money, I had no end of friends willing to leech off me, that is, if I could supply their drinks and drugs for them."

All the color drained from Aaron's face. He had the look of someone who had been punched. He held up a hand for Gene to stop. "Wait a minute, you're trying to tell me that you drank and did drugs back then? There is no way, old man. You do not look like a stoner."

Gene nodded his head. "To my shame, it is true. I am still grateful to this day that God stopped me just short of sticking a needle in my arm, but yes, I was into the drugs. I lied, cheated, stole, and even betrayed others just so I could keep myself partying. I thought that this was a success. I thought I had the attention and the friends I had always desired. I had money; I was successful at my job. I had no shortage of female companionship. In short, by the world's standards, I was what I referred to as a golden boy."

Aaron rubbed his face and when he looked back at Gene, he gave Gene a skeptical look. "I just cannot see you as a party animal, blowing and going. You just are not the type."

Gene held his hands over his head for a moment, looked up to heaven, and said, "I am not the type now not because of anything that I have done but because God saved me from myself again and brought me back onto His path for my life."

Aaron stood up and started to pace. "Come on you expect me to believe that? No one changes like that. No one changes their spots that radically. We are who we are, and that's that."

"Please," Gene said as he motioned for Aaron to resume his seat, "allow me to finish and you will see that nothing is impossible when we are talking about God. Jesus told His disciples that with man, this is impossible, but with God, all things are possible. This is in Matthew 19:26. You see, Aaron, man tries to limit God's power and glory so that they feel more comfortable so that they do not feel uneasy or threatened. Because make no mistake, there will come a day when God will judge the world. So if humans say God doesn't exist or He is not who He says He is then we have no reason to fear Him."

Gene took another sip of water and set the bottle down again.

"God had given me every opportunity to return to the path He had for my life and the relationship with Him that I was neglecting. However, God knew what it would take, and even though He knew, He still sought for me to come back to Him without bringing the hammer down. As I have said, I was stubborn. So as I approached ten years of living like a heathen, God began to remove everything that was a distraction to me. He removed my job, which removed the money, and in turn, removed the so-called friends as there was no reason left for them to hang around, and I was brought to poverty. He removed everything from me that stood in the way of me hearing His voice."

Aaron's thoughts turned to punishment. "Sounds like to me that God was punishing you for disobeying Him."

Gene shook his head. "Most people that I have told my story come to the same conclusion. God would have been justified even if He struck me down. I was deserving of punishment, but God forgives because of His Son, Christ Jesus, remember. This was not punishment; this was God reaching out and as gently as He could to bring me back to Him."

Aaron said, "It sounds like punishment to me. I mean you lost everything. How can you say that God was saving you? You had everything."

Gene shook his head. "No, I had nothing, but back then, I saw the world in a similar fashion to the way you do now. So instead of humbling myself before God, I lashed out in anger at Him.

Aaron got up and started pacing again. "Wait, you lashed out in anger at God? Doesn't God like to throw lightning bolts at those that tick Him off?" Aaron was making fun of Gene now and he could see that Gene knew it. Gene raised an eyebrow at Aaron as if to say, *Do you want to hear the rest?*

Aaron kicked his foot at the floor like a little boy that had been gotten on to and said, "So how did you lash out at God?"

Gene took a moment to gather himself, this was always the most difficult part of his testimony. "I thrust my right fist up toward heaven, shook it, and screamed, why have done this to me? I was enraged."

Aaron plopped back down in the seat, despite his misgivings, he had to admit he was into the story now. He tried to curtail his enthusiasm when he spoke but could not. "So you basically challenged God. Well, what happened old man, what happened?"

Pain remembered flowed across Gene's face as he explained. "God had been speaking to me for years, but I could not hear His voice because of all the sinful distractions in my life, but now all of those had been removed, and I once again could hear my Savior's voice. In a calm, loving, peaceful voice, the Holy Spirit asked this question. What makes you think I did this to you?"

Gene looked up and saw the impact his words had on Aaron. Aaron looked as if someone had gut-punched him, and he was barely breathing.

"When I heard the question," Gene continued. "I dropped to my knees and began to cry. All the guilt, shame, humiliation, and pain of what I had been doing to myself came crashing down on me. I knew exactly who had done this to me, and it had not been God. It had been my decisions and my foolishness that had led me to this point. I also knew that God had been trying to save me from myself the whole time. I knew that He still loved me and wanted what was best for me. I lifted my head to heaven and prayed, 'Father, what do I need to do to make this right? What do I need to do to repair my relationship with you?' That same peaceful voice said, 'Obey me in one thing that I tell you to do, and I will bless you more than you can ever imagine. What is that one thing, Lord?' I asked. 'Go home,' the Holy Spirit told me. Two hours later, I was on my way back to my hometown."

Aaron's head slumped for a moment. The emotional impact of Gene's story was real, and he could not deny it. Then a thought flashed into his head, and he snapped his head back up.

"Hold on, old man, you just admitted that God removed all of what you called distractions, so God did punish you. He took away all your wealth, your job your friends. Explain to me why you think that is the action of a loving God."

Aaron was on his feet again, almost hollering at Gene. He had him, and he knew he did.

Gene smiled, it was an easy smile, the kind of smile that a man has when he has peace.

"God removed those things because He loves me. God knew that if I stayed on that path, I was going to destroy myself. God had much better plans for my life. I may have had material things, but I was in torment, I was never at peace, and I was constantly looking over my shoulder to see where the knife in the back was going to come from. I was scared, paranoid, and so lost that it took God's love to bring me back to a place of love, peace, and joy."

The look that Aaron shot Gene was skeptical. "You had everything I have been trying to get for years. How? Why would you throw it away like that? You lost everything," the last Aaron had screamed at Gene. Gene knew that Aaron was struggling with what he saw as valuable and what God saw as valuable. Gene's gift kicked into overdrive, and he knew the battle was at its peak.

Gene walked over to Aaron, put a gentle hand on Aaron's shoulder, and said, "No, my friend, I gained more than I had ever had in my life.

Aaron had flinched at Gene's touch, was the man getting ready to attack him? Aaron relaxed though when he looked up into Gene's blue eyes, he did not see any threat there, he saw true peace, true love, true joy.

Gene continued with his story. "You see, Aaron, within three weeks, I had another job. Within three months, I met my future wife. Three years after meeting her, I married her, and she has been the love of my life. God blessed us as we went to places I never thought I would go, and we witnessed people across the world. I went back to school and got two degrees. I began teaching at a university, I began to write. In short, I started to live the life that God had always intended for me. When the government began outlawing Christianity, my wife and I took the people we knew were Christians, and we found places where we could be safe and still worship and more importantly, continue to witness to those that were still lost. No, my friend, God did not punish me. He put my feet on the path that was the best for me."

Aaron continued to stare at Gene. He watched for any sign of deceit, any sign that what Gene was telling him was untrue, any sign that Gene really thought God had punished him. He saw none of that. Instead, what he saw was a man pouring his heart out to a person who just an hour ago had been torturing him. Aaron dropped his head in shame and sank to his knees.

Gene dropped to one knee so he could look into Aaron's eyes.

"Aaron, I know that you have always thought that if you could get enough money and power you would never have to be hurt again. No one would be able to abuse you again, and no one would be able to get close enough to damage you more, but I am telling you the money and power that you seek pale in comparison to the life that God wants you to have. He not only wants to bless you in this life, but He wants you to have life eternal in His kingdom in heaven."

Aaron started to shake. The man was sobbing. When he had enough air in his lungs between sobs, the words exploded out, "I don't know how to do what you are asking of me. I have done too much wrong in this life for God to forgive."

Aaron had collapsed on the cold concrete floor of the warehouse from the force of the sobs. Gene sat down next to him and held Aaron in his arms.

"There is not enough wrong in the world that God cannot forgive. As far as what to do, you do not have to know because I do, and I am here to guide you as God always intended," Gene said.

"How?" Aaron asked.

Gene took a deep breath. *Okay, Father, here we go*, and he said a short prayer for Aaron.

"Aaron, do you want to know the Lord Jesus Christ as your personal Lord and Savior? Do you want the forgiveness of God?"

Aaron tried to speak but could not, so he nodded his head.

"Then pray to him. Tell him you are a sinner and need his forgiveness. Repeat after me," Gene said, and he raised Aaron's head so Aaron could see him.

Tears streaked Aaron's face, and he was a man that was broken.

"Lord Jesus, I am a sinner, and I want to give my life to you and make you the Master of my life. Come into my heart, save me from myself, help me to know you. In Jesus's name, I pray. Amen."

Between great racking sobs, Aaron repeated the prayer word for word. When he said amen, his sobs stopped, and his face changed from a tortured soul to one that could see a whole new world opening before him. Tears continued to flow down his face, but now they were tears of joy. Where there had been hatred, there was now love. Where there had been pain and suffering, there was now joy and peace.

Aaron slowly rose to his feet. "I never knew. I never thought. What is happening to me, old man?"

The *old man* name that Aaron had once used derogatorily now was said as a term of endearment and respect.

Gene rose to his feet. Tears of joy streamed down Gene's face, and he hugged his new brother in Christ. "You are saved, my brother, what is happening to you is that for the first time in your life, you are feeling God's love for you. You are experiencing His peace, His joy, His mercy, His grace, and it is overwhelming. God's love is pure, endless, and unconditional. Once you accept Christ as your Savior, you are reborn a different creature. The old Aaron is gone. The person who stands before me now is my brother in Christ."

Aaron slid out of Gene's hug but still held onto his shoulders.

"Lord Jesus?" Aaron asked. "Is that You?" Aaron and Gene heard the smiling laughing reply.

"Yes, my son, it is I. Welcome to the family."

Aaron just stood there, a look of utter amazement on his face.

Gene laughed and said, "Praise You, Lord Jesus, praise You for You are worthy of praise."

# CHAPTER 17

## Aaron the Christian

Aaron stood there, first looking at Gene, then looking around the dingy broken-down warehouse. Only seconds had passed. However, what had happened in those few seconds, Aaron was still struggling to grasp.

One minute he was trying to torture the location of the rest of the believers out of Gene, and one minute he hated everything that the old man stood for and was trying to do everything in his power to bring his world down.

One minute he had decided that he was just going to kill the old man and be done with it. The next he started listening to the old man. He listened to his testimony. He listened to the way God saved him and blessed him.

Some part of him screamed that he should cover his ears and run away. It is all a lie part of him screamed. That part of him was terrified like a trapped animal that knew its days were numbered. There were screams of anguish that accused and insulted Aaron. *Stupid boy*, Aaron heard his father's voice. *You will never be anything*, Aaron heard his uncle's voice. *I never wanted you or loved you*, he heard his mother's voice. *You're throwing it all away, you idiot*, Aaron heard all of them say.

However, through all of that, he heard Gene's story of salvation. He heard a calm, peaceful voice telling him that he was loved, wanted, valued, and most of all, forgiven if he just accepted the gift of salvation.

At some point, Aaron reflected. He had fallen to his knees, he was sobbing, and he could not remember the last time he had cried. Aaron heard a last protest come out of his lips, something about sinning too much to be forgiven, and then not knowing how to do what Gene wanted him to do. God has provided Gene for these moments in Aaron's life. He put Gene here so that Aaron had someone to guide him.

When Gene told Aaron to pray after him, Aaron eagerly prayed as his voice would allow him. He was in so much pain that it felt like his body and soul were being ripped apart and put back together again.

Aaron prayed, and when he said amen, all pain was gone. Aaron could never have imagined this level of love, peace, joy, and forgiveness. He had never known this level of pure unadulterated acceptance in all his life. It was like a fountain spewing forth, and the well of his soul could not contain it. Tears of joy streamed down his face.

"Lord Jesus?" Aaron asked. "Is that you?" Aaron and Gene heard the smiling and laughing reply.

"Yes, my son, it is I. Welcome to the family. You will never walk alone again. You are a new creation, my creation, and you are loved."

Aaron stood there vibrating with energy. He had never felt so alive. He had never felt so hyped in all his life. He had to do something, but what? He spun around several times and then thrust both hands in the air above his head and said, "Thank You, Lord Jesus, thank You."

Aaron didn't know if this was what he was supposed to do, he just felt so much gratitude.

He stopped, faced Gene, and said, "Uncle Gene."

Gene smiled. All his flock called him Uncle. Aaron had no way of knowing this, except through the Holy Spirit, which now indwelled in Aaron.

"Yes, nephew."

"What do I do now? I can't stay here." Then another thought occurred to him. "Oh no, but more importantly you can't stay here. I must get you out of here."

Aaron began running around the table picking up things he thought they would need to get Gene out of this building. He picked up his knives, which he had dropped on the floor at some point. He picked up his gun, he put on his coat and gloves.

Gene walked over, placed a hand on Aaron's shoulder, and turned him.

"We have some time before we depart. I would tell you some things about your new life."

Aaron smiled. He was anxious to hear what Gene had to say, but he was afraid that if Gene stayed here one more moment something awful might happen to him and Aaron would not allow that.

Gene saw Aaron's fear for him and was touched by it. However, one of the first things Aaron needed to learn was to rely on God's plan and timing. Gene knew that Aaron had made his way in this life through his wits and always having a plan. He had to teach Aaron that for the first time, he had to relinquish this control to God.

Gene gently pushed Aaron into a chair at the table, then he sat opposite him. He looked his former torturer in his eyes.

"My brother, for we are now brothers in Christ. You must learn a few things to start with before we can leave."

"What things?" Aaron almost screamed the question. His fear for Gene was real. "You don't know these people as I do, they will kill you, and I cannot allow that."

Gene smiled. "Aaron, I know these people. God gives me my gift of insight. Let me ask you a question. Do you think that God saves us and then just abandons us to flounder around?"

Aaron looked at Gene with genuine concern and confusion.

"The answer is no, He does not. You are a new creature, Aaron. You have the Holy Spirit of the living God in you. You must learn to listen to God, trust God, and obey God. God's will is perfect. God does not make mistakes. If it is God's will that we get out of here, then God will give us what we need to do that, but before that happens, you need to understand who you serve now."

Aaron's face was at peace now as Uncle Gene spoke. There was something about the man's words and tone that just put you at ease. An unbidden question popped into Aaron's head.

"How do I learn to listen, trust, and obey?"

Again, Gene smiled and tapped Aaron on his forehead.

"Love the Lord your God with all your heart, all your mind, with all your body, and all your soul. In other words, with everything you are. Next, read the Bible, God's Holy Word, to us. Along with that, spend quiet time with God every day. Allow your relationship with God to grow by doing this. Next, put your complete trust and faith in God. Do not trust what others can do for you. Do not trust what you can do for you. Trust that God has a plan for your life, and He will fulfill that plan. Also, you are part of a whole now. Just as there are many parts to the human body, but all the parts do not serve the same function, so too it is with other Christians, we are of one body, but we do not all serve the same purpose. Finally, Ephesians 4:22–24 teaches us, about your former life, put off your old self, that self is corrupt by its deceitful desires; be made new in the attitude of your mind, and put on the new self, created to be like God in true righteousness and holiness. When you spend your quiet time with God, it is easier to shake off the old self and put on the new self. Be mindful my brother that just because you are God's now, does not mean that you will not be tempted to embrace your old self. Rely on God for your strength to resist these temptations and stay on the path that he has for you."

Gene patted Aaron on his knee. "Do you understand?"

Aaron gave Gene a doubtful look and answered honestly. "Some yes but not all, it is a lot to take in."

"Good," Gene said as he rose to his feet. "That is a good place to start. Not to worry, you have God and a whole lot of brothers and sisters who will help you understand. Remember, you are no longer alone in this world."

Aaron stood and smiled. "That part I understand, and I am thrilled by it."

"Outstanding," Gene exclaimed. "Now we can leave."

"Good," Aaron said with a sigh of relief. Here is what I think we should do. I will go out first. I will leave the door open behind me. I will head to the south. That way leads to the guard post that has the most distance between the other guard posts. We are less likely to attract unwanted attention. I will take out the guard, he will not suspect me, and then you follow along after I have taken care of him. Got it?"

Gene shook his head. "While it is a very well-thought-out plan, and I have no doubt it would work. There is a simpler way."

Aaron's brow furrowed in skepticism. "Okay, Uncle, what is your plan?"

"Well, if you can get that grate in the floor open, we can take the path through the sewers that God revealed to me through one of my flock."

Aaron placed a hand on his face and shook his head in disbelief. "You mean to tell me you had a way out of here and did not take it?"

Gene gave a shrug of his shoulders. "God was not ready for me to leave. He wanted me to bring you with me."

Aaron smiled and then laughed. "Do you always do what God tells you to do old man?"

Gene thought about that question for a moment and answered with humility. "I am by no means perfect, but I try and thankfully God forgives me when I fail and never gives up on trying to make me better."

Aaron bent down and began to lift the grate on the floor. Gene reached down and applied his muscles to the task as well. With a scrapping of metal and rust, the grate began to give.

Through a grunt of effort, Aaron said, "You are amazing, old man."

Nope," Gene grunted in return, "God is amazing. I just happen to be the recipient of His blessings."

The grate gave way and the two men let it drop to the concrete floor. The clang rang like a church bell being rang.

A ladder led down into the darkness. Aaron pulled a flashlight from his belt and shined it down the hole. He then handed another flashlight to Uncle Gene. Gene turned it on and shined a light down the hole as well.

"Age before beauty," Aaron joked, and Gene gave him a look and began his descent.

As Aaron placed his foot on the first rung of the ladder, a thudding came from outside the main door.

"What's going on in there?" Aaron shuddered, the voice was none other than Sloan, and judging by the sound of the pounding on the door and his voice, Sloan was none too happy.

"Time to pick up that pace, Uncle. We've been discovered."

# CHAPTER 18

## The Pursuit

Sloan pounded on the door.

He had returned from his clandestine meeting about thirty minutes ago. He had gone looking for Aaron, but everyone said Aaron was in with the Christian. At first, Sloan didn't think anything about this. After all, Aaron was supposed to be extracting information from the old man. However, as the minutes dragged by, Sloan became increasingly paranoid. What if Aaron already had the information and had decided to reap the whole reward for himself instead of sharing the loot? Sloan could not shake the feeling that he was being betrayed. After all, that is exactly what Sloan was doing to Aaron. What if Aaron had already pulled the trigger for his betrayal? Sloan could not take it anymore, he had to find out what was going on in that warehouse.

Sloan put his ear to the warehouse door. He had to find out what was going on. He heard sounds of subdued speaking, talking in low tones, and once he thought he heard sobbing. He nodded his head; it made sense that there would be sobbing. He had seen Aaron work before. The fact that the old man was sobbing could mean that he had given the location of his followers to Aaron. If Aaron came forward quickly with that information, then Sloan could hold his plans off a bit.

Then Sloan heard something that he had never expected to hear. Both men were sobbing and laughing. This did not make sense at all to Sloan. He waved over to one of the patrols. The two men increased their pace and stopped in front of him.

"You." He pointed to the one on his right. "Go get a crowbar or anything you can find to pry the lock off this door."

The man froze for a minute, unsure if he should follow Sloan's orders. Aaron had told them he did not wish to be disturbed. The man's mind was made up for him when a swift backhand across his cheek sent him staggering toward the main building. He ran to obey.

Sloan returned to listening at the door. He heard a slight movement. It sounded like metal being ground against metal. He pressed his ear even closer and heard grunts of exertion, then a clang of metal on concrete. The last sound was loud, and Sloan jerked away from the door. What could that have been? What was in the building that could have made that sound? Then Sloan remembered the grate on the floor. That was the sound of that grate being removed.

*No!* his brain screamed, and his anger and frustration boiled over.

Sloan pounded on the door.

The guard came back with a crowbar and began to pry the door open. Sloan snatched the crowbar from the man's hands and wedged it in between the clasp and the wood. Within moments, the clasp popped from the door with a loud ping, and Sloan threw the crowbar over his shoulder as he slid the door aside.

Sloan ran to the opposite side of the warehouse. One glance around told him all he needed to know. The old man was gone, Aaron was gone, the grate in the floor had been lifted out of the hole it covered. They had escaped through this grate, and Aaron had assisted in helping the old man escape. This meant that the old man's hocus pocus message had done its work. Aaron, the fool that he is, has been taken in by this charlatan.

Sloan knew who was on the winning side though and he would never allow himself to listen to such malarkey. Every sane person knew that there was no God. It was just a way for old white men to control the population. That message was taught in all the public schools and universities, by the best and brightest the country had to offer, so it had to be true.

*I will kill Aaron slowly for this,* Sloan thought as he allowed the anger to course through him.

Sloan screamed, "Spread the word, fan out, look for the old man and Aaron. Aaron has turned traitor to our group and the state. Find him now."

The two men standing there immediately ran outside and began to wake the camp. The news of Aaron's betrayal and assisting their golden goose to escape spread like wildfire. In minutes, the whole camp was searching for the two escaped men.

Sloan spat and began climbing down the ladder. "I'm coming for you, Aaron. We are all coming for you. You are a fool, and you seriously allowed this old man to convince you that some all-powerful being cares for you?"

As Sloan's feet touched down at the bottom he paused, he looked one way, then the other. Which way did they go? He turned as a breeze touched his face. He smiled a toothy evil smile and ran in the direction the breeze had come from.

"I know which way you went fool, and I am coming to kill you."

The night was chilly and here by the docks, the air carried a dampness to it. Both men drew their arms around their chests to ward off the cold wet air. Aaron looked around, quickly gaining his bearings as to where they had come out. They were behind the camp. That was the good news. The bad news was that Aaron had assigned a patrol on this side of the camp, as there had been a rash of people sneaking in from this area and stealing from them.

"Where now?" asked Gene.

"Well, we can make our way out of the docks if we go northwest, but there is a patrol from the camp that way. It should not be much of a problem to get by them since they will be unaware of my change of heart but keep your wits about you. There are others out here as well that are none too fond of me or my former group."

Gene nodded and fell in behind Aaron as they began their trek out of danger.

They had only gone perhaps a hundred yards when they heard Sloan's scream of vengeance.

The scream had come from the tunnel they had just come out of so there was no doubt that Sloan knew the route they had taken.

"Damn," Aaron swore. "So much for speed and bluffing our way through. Now we must rely on stealth."

Both men ducked behind a mound of garbage.

Aaron glanced around considering the best path to take to avoid the patrol and throw Sloan off their trail. He saw a path that took them through the piles of debris and garbage. It would be slow going, but with any luck, it would keep prying eyes from observing their movements.

He nodded his head and spoke in a whisper to Gene, "This way, Uncle."

Both men moved out at a crouch mustering as much speed as they dared.

Gene followed, but he was saying a silent prayer as well. *Father, thank You for your rescue, thank that Aaron has accepted Your gift of salvation. Father, guide us from the clutches of our enemies.* It then struck Gene that Aaron had begun to call him uncle, as the rest of his flock always had done. Gene smiled and shook his head in amazement at what God was capable of. Under his breath, Gene murmured, "You never cease to amaze me even after all these years, Father."

"What was that?" Aaron was focused on their path, but his senses were heightened.

"Oh, just giving thanks is all," Gene replied.

It was then that another bellow came from behind them.

"I am going to enjoy using your own knives to torture and kill you, Aaron. Maybe I will allow each member of the camp to carve away skin as a souvenir. Maybe I will auction off those chunks. Then again, maybe I will just turn you over to the authorities and allow them to have a go at you."

"Are you okay?" Gene asked in a whisper.

A soft chuckle came from Aaron. "Yes, if he is bellowing and threatening, I know that Sloan has not found evidence of our trail. It is when he goes silent that we need to begin to worry."

Then Aaron heard another bellow from Sloan.

"Aaron…oh, Aaron…I am getting closer, Aaron…I am."

The bellow cut off, and Aaron knew that Sloan had found some clue as to the direction they had gone.

"Now we worry, old man, quickly now."

The two were still crouched behind stacks of junk, but they moved faster now. Aaron's sense of being hunted buzzed in his being. Adrenaline pumped into him, and his senses became aware of every sound, sight, smell, and movement. He calculated that he had gained another fifty yards on Sloan, but now they had run out of debris to hide behind. They had a forty-yard sprint ahead of them to get to the next stacks of garbage. Aaron and Gene paused to catch their breath.

Sloan had gone silent. Aaron knew the man had found their trail. If he was the one that was doing the pursuing, he would get to the highest mound and watch. Both he and Sloan knew the area well. Given the path That Aaron and Gene were taking it was very possible that Sloan would position himself to watch this passage. However, there was nothing for it. Aaron knew that if they stayed put, then search parties would eventually find them. The only chance they had was to run to the next bit of cover and lose their pursuer again.

Aaron drew in a deep final breath and tensed to lunge out of cover and make the dash. Just as his legs twitched to spring into action, he felt a firm yet soft grip on his shoulder.

The touch instantly calmed him, and Uncle Gene said, "Wait, not yet."

Aaron almost took off anyway, but something was telling him to listen to the old man, so he waited.

Moments passed, it felt like an eternity. Every part of Aaron's being screamed to be gone, yet he was determined to follow Uncle Gene's lead.

Then another voice boomed out into the night. "Sloan, have you found them?"

Sloan had made his way to the tallest mound of debris and garbage that he could find. He stared at the open expanse that he knew Aaron and the old man would have to traverse. Once he saw them, he could easily catch up to them by running down the mound. Also, he knew that he had people coming in from the other side. They were trapped. All he had to do was wait until they showed themselves.

A voice from the bottom of the mound boomed up at him. His head instinctively went to the sound. Anger poured out of Sloan as he responded to the idiot who had just given his position away.

"No, you idiot, and shut up. If I had found them, would I be up here staring off into space looking for them? I swear you have the brains of a gnat. If you have caused me to lose them, I will gut you like a fish, idiot."

As soon as the shouted question came from behind them, Gene gave a shove to Aaron's shoulder. Aaron did not have to be able to read minds to know that this was their chance. Both men took off like rabbits being chased by a wolf.

Aaron considered himself fast and the adrenaline made him even faster, yet he was surprised that Uncle Gene was only two steps behind him as they dashed toward the next bit of cover.

Just as they heard Sloan call the man an idiot for a second time they slid behind cover and were once again hidden from their pursuers.

They took a moment to catch their breath once again.

"That was lucky," Aaron whispered.

Gene chuckled again softly and said, "Oh, Aaron, you have much to learn my brother as to how God works. That was not luck, that was God."

Aaron did not know what to believe, but he had seen some amazing things since meeting Gene, so he would take it on faith that God had provided a distraction. They still were not out of the woods yet. It would only take Sloan a few minutes to realize that he had missed their run. Then he would attempt to surround them. Aaron did not know how to prevent this. He had counted on getting away before the alarm had been raised. Now that Sloan and the camp were actively hunting them, Aaron had severe doubts about even his ability to get them out of alive.

Both began moving through the debris, taking care to be as silent as they could. Both could hear other people moving through the debris on all sides.

After about three minutes, from their sprint, they heard Sloan. "Close in from every side. They're in there somewhere. You hear that,

Aaron? I know you are in the junk, and I have men on all sides. You're done!"

Aaron gave a huge sigh of frustration. "He's right you know since we did not make our escape unnoticed. We probably will not make it out of here."

Gene looked around and had to admit that the situation was not good, yet God had gotten him out of worse situations, and he had to trust that God had his back.

"Oh, my new brother, you will see God never abandons his people. He will provide a way. He still has work for me, and your work is just starting, so have faith."

Aaron looked at Uncle Gene with amazement. They were on the run, surrounded by people who at best wanted to turn them into the government, and at worst wanted to kill them outright, and still, the old man knew that they would survive.

"I do not mind telling you that I am frightened, and I have not been that in a long time. Has God shared with you just how He plans to pull our butts out of the fire here? Because I would love to hear it."

Gene smiled. "It is going to be up to you. Right now, there is still doubt amongst your former followers. None of them truly trust Sloan. However, they still may trust you."

Aaron thought about that for a moment. "I suppose, I am a good liar when I want to be, but should I be lying? Won't God frown on that?"

"What lies? The old man you were holding has escaped—truth. Sloan is trying to kill you—truth. You need a diversion so you can avoid being killed by Sloan—truth."

Aaron's mouth dropped open in surprise for a moment, then he responded. "I never would have thought of you being capable of such cunning."

Again, Gene gave Aaron a smile and a shrewd wink. "You will find that God provides for us. While God does not deal in lies, Jesus tells us in Matthew 10:16, 'I am sending you out like sheep among wolves. Therefore, be as shrewd as snakes and as innocent as doves.'"

Again, Aaron was stunned by this. "You mean to tell me that Jesus told us that over two thousand years ago?"

"Yes, Jesus knew what the future held for His followers. He warns us throughout His Word about how men will be in the end times, and He gives us the instructions we need to survive so that we may continue to spread the Good News of our salvation through Christ."

They began to creep through the debris again. They had gone maybe twenty yards when they heard two people ahead of them. Aaron tensed, and Gene hid himself behind a tall and dark pile of garbage.

As he melted into the shadows, he whispered, "Shrewd as snakes, innocent as doves."

Aaron stopped crouching and stood tall as he rounded the bend to confront his former allies. There were two of them. They skidded to a halt as they saw Aaron walking toward them.

They were in ragged jeans and T-shirts, and their shoes had seen better days. The first was short yet muscular with a crooked nose and a scar running over his right eyebrow. His black hair blended into the night. Aaron knew him as Wonky, a nickname, of course, one he had gotten because of his crooked nose. The other was only slightly taller with brown hair, a slight build, and a skeptical look on his face. His name was Shawn, but he went by the moniker of Sus because he rarely trusted anyone or anything.

"Stop," Sus said.

Aaron continued to walk toward them. They both drew knives and went into a defensive stance. Aaron casually stopped about three feet from them.

"You are coming with us, Aaron. Sloan told us to bring you to him."

Aaron shook his head. "Of course, he wants you to bring me to him. He wants to kill me."

"Why does he want you dead?" Sus asked.

"Isn't that obvious?" Aaron countered with his own question.

Sus thought about this for a moment. "Well, he has always said he would take over at some point."

Aaron pushed now. "Look, Sloan has made his move, and he wants me dead. I am trying to avoid being killed. All I need is a little diversion, a little time to get away so I can avoid that. Do you think you, boys, can help me out?"

Sus's suspicious nature kicked into high gear. "Why should we do that?"

Aaron spread his arms wide to show he was not armed. A gesture of peace. "Haven't I been good to the group? Haven't I always made sure you had enough food and clothing? Haven't I always put the group first? Ask yourselves if Sloan is in charge, who do you think he will put first, the group or himself?"

The two men lowered their knives a little. "You have a point there. You have been good to us, and Sloan is a greedy toad who only cares about himself."

"So, gentlemen, my fate is in your hands. Are you going to help in killing me or will you help me escape and put a crimp in Sloan's plans?"

The two looked at each other and Wonky nodded at Sus. They both sheathed their knives, and Sus asked, "What do you need from us, Aaron?"

Aaron shook both men's hands. "My thanks, I need a diversion. Run in the opposite direction of where I am going and holler that you have seen me on the other side of the camp. Pull the net away from me. I will make my escape, but I will come back and try to save you from all of this."

Sus looked at Aaron. He saw no deception in the man. "You better."

The two men went in the opposite directions and, when they had gone far enough away, started screaming that they had found their prey.

# CHAPTER 19

## Cast the Nets

Jonathan made his way out of the garbage-laden docks. He knew he was following God's will, but the fact that he had left his mentor, friend, and brother in those circumstances roiled inside of him. Several times during his trek back to a more familiar part of the city, he stopped, turned, and began to go back. Each time he did this a sense of wrong overwhelmed him, followed by a sense of peace for Uncle Gene.

Jonathan knew that this was the Holy Spirit once again, telling him that he was on the right path. As Jonathan approached the marketplace, a vision of hundreds of fishing nets being cast out filled his mind.

The calm peaceful voice of the Holy Spirit spoke, "Cast the nets and bring my missing flock home."

Jonathan understood. Lord if you just tell me where to go I will go and bring them home, Jonathan prayed silently.

This time when God spoke there was a hint of rebuke, but still peaceful and loving as well. "Why is it that you must question every command that I give? The nets are people who will not just catch your new and old brothers but others as well. I have made you fishers of men. Cast the nets, send out believers so that they may fulfill their purpose by saving others from eternal damnation."

Jonathan felt the weight of God's voice upon him. He fell to his knees and began to pray.

"Lord Jesus, please forgive me for my questioning. Help me, Lord, to listen, trust, and obey. I will do as you say. I will gather our community of believers. I will cast out the nets, and we will be catchers of men."

God did not speak to him again, but Jonathan got a sense that God was smiling at him. Uncle Gene and God had taught him that no matter how many times you mess up, God's love, mercy, and grace are sufficient. Once again God forgave Jonathan and once again, Jonathan was amazed. Jonathan's feet seemed to float; he was energized like he had never been before.

He began to run. He was not far from the market, so he arrived quickly. The day was waning, so there were not many people there. The streets and alleyways that made up the market were indeed bare. However, it did not escape Jonathan's notice that most people who were still there were known to him as believers in Christ. Not all, of course, so he would have to be careful.

Jonathan slowed as he approached Kyle's tables. The portly man with the clean-shaven jovial face, looked concerned. His brow was furrowed, and his lips were drawn tightly together. As he saw Jonathan, he leaned forward and spoke in a quiet voice as Jonathan came within earshot.

"Jonathan, what has happened?" The question was fraught with anxiety as the words spewed forth in a rush.

Jonathan held his right hand out and patted at the air, indicating to remain calm. Kyle tried to calm himself, but he knew that something was wrong and found it difficult to keep himself from grabbing the young man by the collar and shaking information from him.

Jonathan leaned against one of Kyle's tables for a moment, then stood up, and began to tell the kind shopkeeper what had happened.

"Uncle Gene has been taken."

"Taken by who?" Kyle blurted out.

Jonathan brought his index finger up to his lips in a gesture of quiet.

Kyle leaned in closer, and Jonathan lowered his voice to tell what he had seen and heard.

"He was taken by a group that seeks to turn Christians in for the price the government has on our heads. Money and power are all they want. This particular group is run by a man named Aaron. He has been torturing Uncle Gene for information. This guy doesn't just want Gene. He wants to know the location of as many followers as possible."

"Oh no," Kyle whispered, "I have heard of Aaron. He is a nasty piece of work. He is not only very good at extracting information, but he is also very smart. He is not your everyday run-of-the-mill heathen."

"From what I saw and heard, I would have to agree with you, my friend," Jonathan said.

Jonathan's body quivered, and his voice broke as he relayed to Kyle his experiences in the sewer lines underneath the warehouse.

Several times during Jonathan's account, Kyle broke in with, "Why didn't you stop them, or why didn't you rescue him?"

After the third admonishment by Kyle, Jonathan shoved the man back and in a lower menacing voice said, "I wanted to, but that was and is not what God wanted. God spoke to me and told me what I must do. I even spoke with Uncle Gene, and he insisted that God had sent him to save Aaron and that I must not interfere. Then God told me to leave, just leave him there, in the hands of our enemies. Do you have any idea how hard that was for me? To just walk away from the man who raised me. To walk away from the man who led me to the Lord."

Tears streamed down Jonathan's young strong face. Kyle reached out a hand and patted him on the shoulder. "I am sorry, my brother. I should have shown you more compassion. I am afraid."

"We are all afraid. This society and culture have become one that is openly hostile to all who follow our Lord Jesus. This world has always been hostile to God. But recently, people hate God and all who follow him. Jesus told us this would happen, and yet He is still with us. Still speaking with us, still guiding us, and still loving us. The truth is, that no matter what this world does to us. In the end, they will acknowledge that Jesus is Lord of lords and King of kings.

Pity those that do not accept Christ Jesus, for in the end, it will be revealed that they have condemned themselves."

Kyle nodded his head and simply said, "Well said, Brother Jonathan, well said."

Jonathan looked up, and his green eyes flashed. "God has not abandoned Uncle Gene or us. He has told me what we need to do. I do not know how, but somehow God is going to get Uncle Gene out of that awful place. Gather all the brothers and sisters in Christ that you can get a hold of and cast the nets."

Kyle stood up straight. "Cast the nets? What does that mean?"

Many in the crowd were inching forward closer to the two men. Some just to hear what was being said, others out of curiosity. At any other time, none would have attempted this because it was dangerous to have so many be in even this vicinity to each other. However, they were being drawn; for whatever reason, most felt the weight, the importance of this conversation, even if they did not hear all of it.

Jonathan smiled. "Send out our brothers and sisters to every avenue that Uncle Gene may take to get back to the market, have them watch and wait. Once one of them discovers Uncle Gene have them bring him to your house. Then we will have to plan on what to do next. Also, let them know that they are to fulfill the great commission that Jesus gave us. They are to witness to those whom they are led to witness to, they are to become fishers of men. God has told me that this night is not just about getting Uncle Gene back, it is about the harvest for God. Many will give themselves to Him tonight."

Kyle swallowed hard. "Jonathan, we put all in danger if we do this. It is dangerous to have so many out and in groups larger than two. Surely there is another way to go about this. A way that does not put so many of us in harm's way."

Jonathan was glad to see that he was not the only one who questioned God's plans. He held up a hand and smiled again.

"Believe me when I tell you that this is a conversation that I have already had with the Holy Spirit. I was told with authority that this is the course of action we are to take. We must trust in God. I am bidden to say this to you and please pass it on to all we summon for this task. If I rise on the wings of the dawn, if I settle on the far side of the sea, even there your hand will guide me, your right hand will hold me fast. This is from Psalms 139:10. God is telling us to trust Him."

Kyle nodded his head in understanding.

Jonathan turned to leave. "Where are you going?" Kyle asked.

Jonathan didn't break stride but said, "I go to prepare Uncle Gene's flock and cast the nets from there. You spread the word here, cast the nets brother, cast the nets."

The brothers and sisters who had seen the interaction between Jonathan and Kyle gathered around Kyle's stalls without having to be told. They knew something was up. Quickly and quietly, Kyle told them what had happened and the plan to cast the nets. There were worried expressions and fear to be sure, yet when Kyle began to divide them up into teams of three, not one of them faltered.

They moved out from the marketplace like nets being cast into the ocean.

# CHAPTER 20

## The Escape

As the two men started raising the false alarm, Aaron waved at Gene in the shadows and said, "Come on, Uncle, time to go."

Gene emerged from the shadows, and he was smiling. As they began to walk quickly toward their avenue of escape, Aaron could not help but ask. "What on earth could there be to smile about, old man?"

Gene looked up at Aaron and around his surroundings. Trash and debris were everywhere. Mounds of trash reached toward the sky. All these separate mounds created a series of paths and avenues, but they also created excellent hiding places. This area of the city had long been forgotten. Yet God's children were still here, still longing to be reconciled with God the Father, even if they did not know it.

"I am smiling because you did not lie."

"What?" Aaron asked incredulously. "You're smiling because I didn't lie?"

"Of course, you could have. It would have been easy to lie to those men. They trust you, and you could have lied to them and put them in even further danger. But you did not, so I am smiling."

Aaron looked at Gene and said, "Still not sure what difference whether I lied or not makes. I just need to get us out of a sticky situation."

The difference is that the Holy Spirit of God lives in you now and is changing you. Your soul longs to be more like your Savior,

Christ Jesus. This is further evidence that you have accepted Christ. Your face has been unveiled, and you are transforming into His image. Praise be unto God."

"What?" whispered Aaron, as he crawled through a particularly ripe section of road. "I am being transformed alright. I am going from only a little dirty and nasty to disgusting and rank."

Gene chuckled a little as he, too, was crawling through the muck, and it was unpleasant.

Gene recited from the Bible, "Second Corinthians 3:18 reveals to us, 'And we all who with unveiled faces contemplate the Lord's glory, are being transformed into His image with ever-increasing glory, which comes from the who is the Spirit.'"

Aaron coughed quietly and then chuckled as well. "Let me get this straight. We are running for our lives, from a psychopath, who wants both of us dead, we have to crawl through the vilest trash to avoid detection, we are both cold, wet, and smell like the back end of a sewage pipe, and you choose this time to point out how I am being transformed?"

Gene smiled and shrugged his shoulders, as Aaron stared back at him.

"Old man, I am not sure at this point whether I love you or hate you." As he said it, there was a smile on his face. "We can stand now, slow and low still though, come on this way."

After about five minutes they put distance between themselves and their pursuers, they broke into easier open terrain and began to move even faster breaking into a jog.

The area was not as congested with garbage. Instead, it was a scattering of debris. The area was not as flat though and both men trudged their way up a sloping hill. They now moved through the ruined outskirts of the former city.

"So far, we have made good our escape, but Sloan doesn't give up so easily. He may have been distracted for a bit, but he will pick up the trail again. We must be well out of here before that happens."

Uncle Gene walked along with Aaron, but the smile never left his lips.

"Again, still smiling. Did you not just hear what I said to you?"

"I did, my young brother in Christ. I use the word *young* as you are showing your immaturity. You see worry such as you are taking part in now is a sign of an immature relationship with our Savior and Lord."

Aaron hung his head.

"Please, Aaron, I do not say that to chastise you. I say it to inform you that you must trust in the Lord. It is an exciting time for you, you will see wonders and miracles, God will show you His power, His mercy, His peace, and He will show you, His faithfulness. Jesus told us He would never leave or forsake us. This is the period that God will show up, show out, and convince you that His promise of never leaving us is true."

"I am sorry, Uncle. This is all so new to me."

"I know, and more importantly God knows. God also knows your talents, strengths, and weaknesses even better than you. He will use the talents He gave you to further His kingdom, protect His flock, and bring joy and peace to others."

"So what do you think God will do to get us out of this?" asked Aaron.

"I have no idea right now," Uncle Gene replied immediately. "That is the exciting thing about it, waiting on God to see how He will show Himself in any given situation."

"Aren't you ever afraid?" Aaron paused, walking as he asked the question.

Gene paused long enough to look at his young friend. "Oh my, yes, all the time. These are horrifying times we are living in. Mostly, I am afraid for my brothers and sisters in Christ. My fear threatens to overwhelm me at times."

They began walking again.

Aaron scratched his head and said, "Why do you think you have so much fear? You do a good job of hiding it."

Gene chuckled. "I am afraid for my brothers and sisters in Christ. You see, I can remember a time when the United States was a place of God-fearing people. There was a time when we revered God and most of our citizens were Christians. We have gone from a nation that supported The Lord's ministry to a country that reviles any who follow Christ. Christians are hunted, tortured"—Gene gave Aaron an ironic look of sympathy—"imprisoned, and even killed. I fear, yet I know I should not. God is in control. God holds each one of us in His hands."

"As far as hiding it well, that is not me. That is God's peace shining through despite my misgivings. God has reminded me more than once that I am His and so is my flock. When I become stubborn and what to do things my way, or I disagree with God, He sometimes gently reminds me and, sometimes not so gently, that He is in control."

"So we do not have any control over our lives anymore?" Aaron's face was contorted in a frown as he asked the question. Gene saw a face he once had. A face that said, *I do not want to be a slave. I want to be able to make my own decisions.*

Gene laughed as the two of them turned a corner, and he found that they were only three blocks away from the market where he was taken. The night had passed, and it was approaching dawn, maybe an hour or two away.

"My brother, we still have free will. It is just now that you are part of the body of Christ, you will want your will and your decisions to match up with the will of God like never before. As your relationship grows, you will have more insight into the will of God, and you will see the right of the decisions that God makes. You are in a relationship with the Creator of the universe, and there will be times when you are asked to do some things that, at the time, make no sense to you. You will be told to do them anyway. It is usually at this point that I have an argument with God."

"Wait," Aaron exclaimed, "you are telling me that you have arguments with God?"

"Yes, not only arguments but there are times I am upset and angry with God. This is a personal relationship with my Lord and Savior Jesus. There are times when I do not understand, or I disagree because of my selfish, sinful nature that I get upset."

Gene could see that hard swallow penetrating Aaron's throat. The last statements frightened Aaron the most. It brought home that when you gave your life to Christ, you were His, and He would always be with you. It dispelled the myths and barriers that man-made religions had spent centuries building. Barriers such as you need a human intermediary to speak to God, that you need a saint to speak on your behalf. Gene never could understand all the man-made rules; all of which, only served to separate us from God. It only convinced him more of what God had revealed to him. Religions are man-made much like the Sadducees and Pharisees had done in Jesus's time; they only made these rules to extort people of their money and, therefore, gain power for themselves.

Gene placed an arm around Aaron as they walked. "My boy, God loved us enough to sacrifice and resurrect His only begotten Son so we could be saved and reconciled to Him. Don't you think His love and forgiveness can survive a disagreement?"

Aaron thought about the old man's words and his mind and spirit eased and was at peace. He felt more loved than he ever had in his life, he understood more than he ever had, and he was more terrified than he ever had been. However, the joy and the peace that was coursing through all of him easily overcame any doubts and fears that he was experiencing as soon as they arose. This was especially true when he was listening to Uncle Gene speak. Aaron realized once again that God was using Gene to teach and prepare Aaron for the mission he was to have for the kingdom. Aaron did not have the slightest idea what that was going to be, but he decided to trust God for that.

A calm, peaceful voice there yet not there said, "Well done, you are learning."

Aaron jerked to a stop. His knees nearly buckled.

Gene instinctively reached out and steadied the young man.

"What is it?" Gene asked anxiously. Gene thought that perhaps Aaron had seen pursuit that he had not seen.

Then through the dimly lit alleyways Gene saw Aaron's face, transform from a look of shock to one of pure joy, and he knew what had happened.

Gene smiled and clapped Aaron on the back. "It is a little unnerving the first couple of times the Holy Spirit speaks to us. I have gotten accustomed to it, but it is always amazing and unexpected."

Aaron's smile could not be contained on his face. As he looked squarely at Gene, he said, "God speaks directly to us?"

Gene patted Aaron on his face and replied, "Why yes, yes, He does. You cannot have a personal relationship with someone if you do not speak with them."

Aaron's face although still full of joy also had so many questions.

"But how…why…do we—" Aaron stammered out these questions, and there were many more, but he could not get them out. His mind was overwhelmed.

Gene gently guided Aaron to sit down. Both men slid down with their backs against a brick wall.

"We will have time to answer and discuss all of your questions. For now, all you need to know is what Jesus told us in John 10:27, 'My sheep know my voice and they will follow my voice.'"

Gene stood up and reached down his hand at the man who had not too long ago been torturing him. "Come, my brother, we are almost to a friend's house. There we will have food and rest."

Aaron took Gene's hand, and it was surprisingly strong for the man's age. The old man pulled him up like he weighed nothing.

Aaron shrugged and said, "Lead the way, old man, lead the way."

# CHAPTER 21

## *Rage*

Sloan's eyes scanned the garbage piles and the shadows that they caused. He forced his breathing to stay even. Any moment now his prey would pop out of those shadows and Sloan would pounce.

Sloan began to fantasize about how he would kill Aaron. He began to imagine what tortures he would inflict upon the foolish old man, and how sweet it would be when the old man gave up the location of the camp.

Sloan then imagined the lavish mansion he would live in, the harem of women he would enjoy, and finally the utter control he would have over those around him. No more would he have to take orders from anyone because he would be the one giving the orders.

Sloan was so deep in his fantasy of control that it took a moment for the shouts to penetrate his conscious mind. However, when they finally did, it brought him crashing down with a harsh blow.

He heard, "Hurry, they've doubled back. They've got behind us."

Sloan jumped down off the pile of garbage. He lost his footing and tumbled down the last ten feet. He rolled and came to his feet as two of his men emerged from the shadows. Sloan could not tell whether they had seen his fall. Not that it mattered, he decided, if either one showed any signs of embarrassing him, he would simply kill both. Sloan was done taking half-measures. He was done being held back by some sense of morality. There was no morality; there was only power. The power to control your destiny and the destiny of others. That was the kind of power Sloan sought and he would have it just as soon as he caught Aaron and the old man.

Sloan ran toward the sound of the report. A few seconds was all it took to get to the open area where his men were gathering and listening to reports of their prey getting away.

Sloan looked and saw Wonky talking. The short man with the muscular build looked like someone displaced in time. He should have been either a Greek or Italian warrior. He sure had the build and the broken nose to fit the bill.

Sloan shoved his way through the gathering crowd and yelled, "What is this all about, Wonky?"

Wonky raised a short stubby arm and pointed south. "Sus and I saw them, sir, the two we are chasing. They've doubled back and are attempting to escape going south."

Sloan thought about this for a moment. It did not make sense that Aaron would go that way. It was more difficult and there was a one-hundred-yard swim through junk filled ocean. However, he thought, perhaps that is why Aaron went that way, perhaps Aaron knew that Sloan would focus his attention on the north, on the easier route.

Sloan's face contorted in anger, then in an evil grin. He pointed at Sus and Wonky.

"You two lead half the men toward the south. Fan out, find me the traitor and the old Christian fool. When you find them bring both to me."

Sus and Wonky moved out to the south, and half of the men followed in their wake.

Sloan's thoughts whirled in chaos. He would have them soon. He would torture and kill them both. He would have the power over not only this group of filth but other gangs as well. As soon as word got out that he had killed Aaron and that he had extracted the location of the Christian camp and brought that threat under control he could have anything he wanted. Sloan was engulfed in his soon-to-be wealth when a thought hit him like a sledgehammer. What if one of these vermin killed Aaron? What if one of these vermin got the information out of the old fool? He could not have that. Everyone had to witness his triumph, everyone had to see that he had beaten Aaron and broke the old man.

"Wait!" Sloan shouted.

The group of men moving with Sus and Wonky stumbled over each other as they obeyed the command. There were shouts of indignation as feet were trod upon and backs were bumped into.

Sloan's eyes glowed with hatred as he spat out into the air. "This is my kill. I will lead us to this triumph."

He pushed through the mass of humanity until he got to where Sus and Wonky were at the head of the group. "Back!" he hissed at the two men. The two men backed up and allowed Sloan to take the lead.

Sloan's stride was that of a conquering general on his way to stamp out the last resistance to his rule. All the while, dreams of his conquest and rule whirled around in his head.

It took fifteen minutes for Sloan and his mob to reach the area where the ocean met the land. Sloan was not the best tracker in the world, but he could read basic signs of passage. He had seen none. This had planted the seeds of doubt.

As he stood at the shore and saw no signs that the garbage floating in the ocean had been disturbed, the seeds of doubt bloomed into complete paranoia and panic.

He turned slowly on Sus and Wonky, his face a mask of controlled rage.

"You two told us they had come this way." His voice was a menacing low growl.

Sus began to answer, but before he could, Sloan had covered the distance between them and had a knife at Sus's throat. He pressed the blade in just enough that blood trickled down the blade and onto Sloan's fingers.

"Think very carefully about the answer to this question, Sus, as it could be the last time you draw breath to speak. Did you and Wonky just lead us on a wild goose chase?"

Sus looked Sloan in the eyes and then craned his eyes to look at the blade. He was terrified by the crazy look in the man's eyes and more terrified by the blade at his throat. However, he did not know what a wild goose chase was.

"I don't understand the question, boss," Sus said, his voice quivering.

The blade in Sloan's hands dug just ever so slightly deeper into Sus's jugular.

Sus wanted to move away from the blade, but he knew it would only take a flick of Sloan's wrist to end his life.

Sloan spat out each word slowly. "Have…you…deceived…me?"

Sus's mind tried to figure out an answer that would not end in his death. If he told the truth, he was dead, if he stuck with the lie, he may be dead. It all depended on how well he could lie. He decided to continue with his and Wonky's story.

"No, boss, we saw them heading in this direction. We could hear them taking some. Aaron said that he knew a way around having to swim through the junk inlet, I swear."

Sloan watched carefully. He couldn't tell whether Sus was lying or not. He slowly lowered the knife, looked at Wonky, and asked, "Is he lying? Before you answer understand that both of you will die if I find out you are lying."

Wonky had been around Sloan long enough to know that if he ratted Sus out, he would kill them both just for kicks, so Wonky also continued the deception.

"We are telling you the truth."

Sloan pointed at several men behind Sus and Wonky. "Subdue them and tie them up. Put them in the warehouse. Once we catch our prey, we will know the truth. If they have told the truth, then they will be released. If not, I will take great pleasure in gutting them."

Five men jumped Sus and Wonky from behind. The two men acquitted themselves well. Even though they were outnumbered and jumped from behind, Sus managed to take out one opponent with a kick to the man's knee, there was a sickening crunch, and the man went down screaming and clutching his right knee.

Wonky sidestepped his first attacker and hit the next one with a roundhouse punch square in the jaw that dropped him to the ground.

He was out before he hit the ground. The attacker that Wonky had sidestepped came at him from behind. Wonky kicked back into the man's groin. There was a whoosh of breath, a barely audible grunt of pain, and the man slid into a fetal position on the ground.

Six more men joined the fray and to their credit, Sus and Wonky were able to incapacitate two more before sheer numbers turned the tide. Sus and Wonky were kicked, punched, gouged, and slapped until they hit the ground.

In the end, Sus and Wonky were bound and gagged.

Both men thought the same thing once they had been subdued. *I hope Aaron was telling the truth. I hope he comes back for us and saves us.*

Sloan walked over and kneeled next to Sus. With a deft flick of his wrist, a knife appeared and lashed out at Sus's face. The blade cut just deep enough on Sus's cheek to make blood flow. Sloan glared hatred at Sus. "Just a taste of what will happen to you if you ever lie to me again." Sloan smiled as he stood.

Sloan motioned to the half of his men to follow him, and they once again took up the pursuit to the north. The other half he instructed to comb the area for any sign of the two fugitives.

Sloan's thoughts were primitive. He knew he had been deceived and he knew that Aaron and the piece of human filth known as Gene had escaped this area. Sloan also knew that he and this group had informants throughout the city and surrounding areas. It was only a matter of time before he had his hands on them. Then he would take great pride in making them pay for this humiliation. He had been going to kill Aaron quickly, but now he would take his time and enjoy every minute of it. Images of cutting into Aaron's flesh until the bone was exposed danced in his head. Sloan smiled as he strode back north.

This was going to be fun. He would show his people and more importantly those in power that he should be hired as the premier Christian hunter. He wanted all of them brought to justice, he wanted all of them strung up. I mean who did they think they were? Everyone knew that God did not exist and that the rhetoric of the Christians was just a way to enslave everyone to their control. All the media, wise ones, and the government said so. In Sloan's case, he really did not care about all of that. He just wanted his, and he wanted to be rich and never have to live in squalor again.

A thought flashed through Sloan's mind. Rogan, if Sloan did not have them back in half an hour, he still had Rogan as a card to play. Granted he would have to share credit with the slimy politician, but there were ways he could deal with that as well. The main thing was he would find Aaron and Gene. He would find them, and then his dream of having control over his life would be fulfilled. He would be revered among the peoples of the nations and those that held real power.

# CHAPTER 22

## Trust in the Lord

The diversion that had allowed Gene and Aaron to escape their pursuers had long since passed and Sloan was doubling his efforts. Three times in the last hour, they had avoided those who were looking for them. Dawn was approaching and they had been on the run all night, so Aaron's nerves were beginning to fray. He was used to facing his problems head-on with his fist, his knives, or simply outwitting his opponents—not running away.

The night had been cool, even cold at times, but a trickle of nervous sweat ran down his cheek as he and Gene hid from a police patrol. Not only were they avoiding Sloan and his men, but they had to avoid the police as well. If they were caught skulking around, they would be taken in for questioning, and that would not be good. Aaron had some connections with the cops, but those would not hold up too long given their circumstances.

Gene and Aaron currently hid in an alleyway, behind some wooden crates. While the smell had improved immensely from the mounds of garbage, the fact that their lives hung in the balance was still the same.

Aaron let out a long silent sigh. He heard Gene chuckle and whisper a prayer.

"What?" Aaron whispered through clenched teeth.

Gene placed a strong aged hand on Aaron's shoulder. "This running and hiding does not sit well with you, my brother. You are accustomed to a more direct approach to handling your problems."

Aaron relaxed some at the old man's touch. He turned his face to look at Gene in the dim light. "Is it that obvious?" Aaron asked sarcastically.

Gene slid his hand off Aaron's shoulder and smiled. "You do not have to be a genius to understand that a man that has spent his entire life, confronting challenges head-on and in most cases with violence would have an issue with skulking in the dead of night."

Aaron smiled at the old man, and then his sharp features snapped into a frown.

Gene eased down into a sitting position; his knees would not allow him to stay crouched for any extended period of time. "Tell me what else is bothering you?"

Aaron leaned forward to peer around the crates. There was still too much activity. For as late as it was, there sure were an awful lot of people roaming the streets. Aaron knew that most likely anyone they ran into had a potential for being caught, so they would have to remain here for the time being.

Aaron also slid down into a seated position beside Gene.

"Okay, since we appear to have some time, I don't mean to question God, but why is it that He does not simply put people in power that treat His people well? I mean surely that is something that God could do. Why allow people that hate Christians into a position where they can hurt those that have been saved?"

Gene scratched his head and gave Aaron a painful, yet resigned expression.

"First, it is good that you ask questions. That question has been asked for ages. God is not willing that any be lost. Yes, God could force things; however, it goes back to God does not want slaves. He wants us to have a relationship with Him. As I told you before, if there is no free will, there can be no true love. Next, God's plan will be revealed to us in His perfect timing."

Gene looked at Aaron's face. He could see that Aaron was struggling, so he continued, "We do not lean on our own understanding but rely on God's understanding. Aaron, you must know that God works so that all that can be saved will be saved. Sometimes that means that those of us who already believe must endure hardships, persecution, and even death."

Aaron winced at that. "I do not like the sound of that," he stated flatly.

Gene's smile was one of sympathy. "None of us do but think about our reward, not the trials that we will go through. God is working on each of us. He is making those of us who already believe in the best versions of ourselves that we can be. In short, He is preparing us for the day that Christ will return. In James 1:1–3, 'God tells us, consider it pure joy, my brothers and sisters, whenever you face trials of many kinds, because you know that the testing of your faith produces perseverance.' Do I wish that we did not have to go through the things that this world puts us through? Of course, but I also know that God is in control, that He is faithful, and that He will finish all good works that He has begun in us."

Aaron nodded.

Gene reached up both hands and turned Aaron's face toward him. He locked eyes with Aaron.

"You are now a soldier in the most important and difficult war that has ever been fought. This is a fight for men's souls. The Bible tells us in Ephesians 6:12, 'For we wrestle not against flesh and blood, but against principalities, against power, against the rulers of darkness of this world, against spiritual wickedness in high places.' Satan's only desire is to doom all he can. He already knows he has lost; he already knows that he cannot win, but he still desires to take all he can into hell. That is how evil our enemy is."

Aaron shuddered, and Gene removed his hands from Aaron's face.

"That is awful," Aaron said.

Gene nodded. "Yes, it is."

"All of this," Gene continued, "is foretold in the book of Revelations in the Bible. The people of this earth will turn their backs on God. Evil will consume the planet when no one else can be saved when all have made their decision of which power to follow.

Christ Jesus will return, and judgment will be passed. Woe to all who do not find His mercy."

A chill ran up and down Aaron's spine. Just a few hours ago, he had been on the wrong side of that judgment. Now he embraced Uncle Gene's words with joy that Christ had saved him.

Aaron peaked around the crate once more. The way was clear, and they could continue their journey.

Both stood and began a quick but steady pace toward the market. Gene had said that if they could get there, they may be able to find help in escaping Sloan.

Aaron leaned around a corner. He saw no one so he pulled Gene after him. They were approaching the next turn when two people turned the corner. Aaron swore under his breath and ran toward them, if he could take them down, he and Gene may be able to escape.

Gene's voice rang out clearly and in a commanding tone. "Stop."

Aaron, although he did not understand why, skidded to a halt. When he did, he looked up at the two men that stood before him. They were shocked and frightened, but their expressions changed when they heard Gene's voice.

The two men covered the distance to Gene and in a rush embraced him.

"Thank God," one said.

The other lifted his hand in the air and said, "Praise Jesus."

Aaron stood for a moment dumbfounded, then laughed. "Friends of ours I take it?"

The three men walked up to Aaron, and with joy radiating from his face, Uncle Gene said, "Indeed, Brother Aaron, indeed."

Gene embraced the two for a moment longer and then broke away. The man on Gene's left spoke first. "Uncle Gene, what is going on? We heard that you had been captured. We heard that you were being tortured."

The man's speech was quiet, but very rapid like the staccato of a drum roll. He stood only five foot four inches but was muscular. His face was smooth lines with a jagged burn scar that ran across his neck at an angle. He had brown hair and brown eyes, but his eyebrows were strange, strange in that they no longer existed, they had been burned off with acid.

Gene always felt a surge of sympathy whenever he saw Fergus Nealy. His scars were the result of what his parents and people did to him once they found out he had become a follower of Christ. Fergus had paid a high price for his faith, but his faith was as strong as anyone Gene had ever met.

"Both true, Fergus, and I would like to introduce the man that was responsible for both of those things. Fergus Nealy meet Aaron..." Gene turned to Aaron and looked perplexed. "It just dawned on me I do not know your last name."

Aaron smiled at Gene. "My full name is Aaron Daniel Bragson."

Gene held out a hand indicating Aaron and began the introduction a second time. "Fergus, this is Aaron Daniel Bragson, my captor and torturer."

Fergus took a step forward toward Aaron.

Uncle Gene's gentle large hand halted Fergus's approach.

Uncle Gene's kind eyes held both men in place. "He is also the reason I escaped, and more importantly he is our newest Christian brother."

Aaron smiled and held his hand out to Fergus. Tentatively at first Fergus took Aaron's hand, then as the truth rolled over both, they embraced in a hug.

The other man was much taller than Fergus. He stood at six foot five inches tall, weighed somewhere around three hundred pounds, and looked as intimidating as you might think. His face had a rounded edge to it, but the scowl that was on his face gave him the look of a man who had no problem ending your life. Clear blue eyes stared back at you and his bald head completed the "I am a giant of a man" look.

He had started to move swiftly when Uncle Gene had introduced Aaron as his captor yet stopped just as quickly when Aaron was identified as a Christian brother.

Uncle Gene turned his attention to the large man. "Aaron, allow me to introduce, Sam Elliot, also known as, Tiny."

Aaron's head snapped back between Gene and Sam. "You have got to be kidding me," Aaron said as he began to chuckle.

Aaron turned to shake Sam's hand and found himself plucked from the ground in a bear hug. The face that had been scowling with menace now held an angelic smile and radiated joy.

As Aaron dangled in the big guy's grip, he heard, "It is always such a joyous occasion when we meet new brothers and sisters." The voice was deep and soothing like the rumble of thunder on a warm spring night.

Aaron drew what breath he could and said, "I agree, and I look forward to meeting many more, that is if I survive this one."

Sam said, "Oh, sorry." Then he placed Aaron's feet gently on the ground.

Fergus stepped back in and began walking back down the street where he and Sam had come from. "You must tell us all that has happened. It is an extraordinary tale to be sure, but we must get off the street first."

"Agreed," Gene said as he and Aaron followed the two men.

They walked for another fifteen minutes, turning this way and that. Aaron had shaken enough tails in his time to understand that Fergus and Sam were being cautious about not revealing where they were going.

Sam paused in front of an old mom-and-pop store, after looking around for a bit, he went around back. Fergus waited until Sam had enough time to get to the back of the store, then produced a key from his pocket. He inserted the key counted to three then turned it. The door opened without a squeak or groan.

Even though the building appeared to be long abandoned, it was well-maintained. There was dust and grime all over, but Aaron could evidence that work had been done to preserve and even improve the building, especially the interior. He got it, they did not care what the outside looked like, it was part of the disguise.

Tiny came in the back door. He walked over to a staircase and pulled a ball on the banister. There was a click and a section of the staircase opened. The opening was at the bottom of the staircase and when examined closer was a door that had been built into the staircase. Tiny reached out and pulled the door toward him. What little light there was revealed a set of stairs going down. Tiny waved his hand to Gene and Aaron.

"After you, gents."

Aaron gave Gene a why not look and descended into the tunnel underneath the staircase.

# CHAPTER 23

## *The Underground*

He had heard the stairwell door close behind him and even experienced a moment of panic as pitch black engulfed him. Tiny had quickly produced a flashlight and the beam of it bounced off the surfaces as Tiny began to make his way down. Aaron was astonished that Tiny's massive frame fit through the passageway, but he did, but only just. Sam brought up the rear of the group, and he also had a light, so their descent had begun.

The start of their descent was like walking down any other set of stairs. If you could ignore the fact that you were going underground. However, after about thirty feet, the wooden stairs, walls, and ceiling gave way to stone. Now you could not ignore that you were under the earth. For the first time in his life, Aaron experienced claustrophobia. It was there and then gone like a wave crashing over him. Aaron estimated that were around twenty to twenty-five feet underneath the house now and probably a good fifteen to twenty feet away from where they had entered the secret stairwell.

At the bottom of the stairs, Aaron found that he stared at a series of tunnels. Seven of them to be exact. They spoke of a small cavern. Some of the tunnels had the chaotic beauty of nature, others the manmade attempt at beauty. They had been carved out of the rock with pickaxes, shovels, and even explosives. Aaron could not help but wonder if his Christian brothers had done this or if the tunnels had existed previously.

Tiny guided them to the third tunnel from the left. It was one of the naturally created caverns and Tiny had to fold himself almost into a ball to get into the entrance. As his guide was making his way through the opening, Aaron asked, "Did Christians make these tunnels?"

Tiny grunted as he stood up, and he entered the main part of the tunnel. "Yes, the ones that were man-made, yes, as a Christian you can never have too many places to hide."

Aaron had only heard Tiny speak twice now, but each time he was struck by the deep resonance of his voice. He had heard a jazz band once, and he remembered how the plucking of the bass was smooth but vibrated in his core. Tiny's voice was like that. It was a voice that could either calm a panicking crowd or cause a riot to get away from it.

Aaron came through the lowered entrance and straightened up his back popped as he did. Tiny looked back and smiled. "The only old one who has never had a problem getting into the tunnels is Uncle Gene." Tiny pointed to the old man coming through and popping up like a jack in the box.

Aaron looked from Uncle Gene to Tiny. "Old, I am not old, I am only twenty-six."

Tiny shrugged his massive shoulders and said, "That's old."

Aaron began to follow Tiny down the tunnel. "How old are you? You must be at least my age."

Tiny laughed. "No way, I'm only sixteen."

Aaron snapped his head again from Tiny to Gene.

Uncle Gene shrugged and nodded his head.

Tiny spoke again, "Uncle Gene tells me that God knew my purpose and so made me grow early and often."

Aaron could not help himself; he had to know. "What is your purpose, Tiny?"

Tiny stopped, turned, and drew himself up to his full height, his frame blocked the passageway, and muscles seemed to pop up from nowhere. "Isn't it obvious, Aaron, I intimidate people when we need to scare people away?" Tiny's voice was now the version that people would start rioting just to get away from.

Aaron considered himself to be a tough guy, and experience had taught him he could hold his own in any scrap, but Aaron couldn't help himself, he flinched away Tiny.

Gene chuckled, put a hand on Aaron's shoulder, and simply said, "Effective, eh?"

Aaron let out the breath he hadn't realized he was holding and responded, "I'll say, you could rent him out as a billboard."

Tiny chuckled and turned, and the group followed him farther deeper into the tunnel.

The tunnel widened so Gene and Aaron could walk abreast. Even Tiny had enough room now to move without scrunching. Something that Tiny had said earlier had stuck in Aaron's mind.

"Uncle Gene, Tiny said earlier that it was always a good thing to have a place that Christians could hide."

Gene nodded his head. "Yes, that is a true statement."

Aaron's face contorted a bit as he wrapped his brain around that. "I get why having a place to hide is wonderful now. All Christians are being hunted now. The world has branded all of us outlaws, subversives, and even crazy people. This only happened recently, and those manmade tunnels have been here for decades, maybe even longer."

Gene smiled, but even in the dim flickering glow of the flashlights, Aaron could see a pained expression on his Christian brother's face.

Gene took a deep breath and explained, "Do you think this is the first time Christians have had to go into hiding?" Before Aaron could answer, Gene continued, "It is not. Even our own so-called churches have hunted our brothers and sisters before. As I told you before, religion is man-made, and man-made things can be corrupted. However, I get ahead of myself."

They had been walking for at least half an hour by Aaron's estimation. The tunnel had contracted and expanded as if the rock itself were breathing. Right now, they were in a bigger part of the tunnel, and Aaron thought he heard echoes of voices in the distance, but it could just be his imagination playing tricks on him. He had not admitted it to anyone, but the tunnels made him uneasy, and he would be glad when he could see the open sky again.

"Jesus told us in Luke 21:19, 'Everyone will hate you because of Me.'

"There are several times in the Bible that Jesus warns us of the world's hatred and ill-treatment of His followers. Another such time is in John 15:19, where he says, if you belonged to this world, it would love you as its own. As it is, you do not belong to this world, but I have chosen you out of the world. That is why the world hates you."

Since the first Christians, the world has hated us, persecuted us, and even killed us. So you see, my friend, what the world is doing to us is nothing new. The justifications that they use may change, but the fear and hatred of us remain the same. The biggest difference this time is that the world's governments, businesses, and media are orchestrating this hatred and fear. It will get worse."

Uncle Gene's hands moved as he spoke and as he spoke, his speech pace and patterns became more animated and impassioned.

"Then, of course, there is Rome. Rome persecuted, hunted, and killed our brothers and sisters. From that time forward, all you must do is look in any Muslim country and Christians have been killed. Different denominations of Christianity have been killed by other Christians."

Gene's speech was so strong that Aaron could see the history. God's holy spirit was showing Aaron the truth. They continued to walk, and Gene's history lesson became full of fire.

"The truth is the world hates us. It hates us because deep down they know that they do not have a relationship with the Creator of the universe. The world hates us because they have been lied to and manipulated by the enemy. The world hates us because, in their pride and arrogance, they will not accept the gift of salvation. They hate us because humans do not need much of a reason to hate. They only need a target to focus that hatred on. The government for years has been giving people that target. People in power want to stay in power. They use fear and hatred to keep them in power. If you listen to any newscast, read any paper, or watch any newsfeed, the message is centered around fear and hatred. They have used those weapons for years. Now it is once again Christians who bear the brunt of that fear and hatred."

Aaron looked at Gene and asked, "You sound as if you hate those who hate you. But doesn't God tell us to love our enemies?"

Gene shook his head slightly. "I don't hate the people. I hate the evil that permeates them. I tell you. I would give my life if only one of them would accept Christ. Otherwise, weep for those who are not saved, and have pity on those who do not know Jesus. For the end is near and it will not go well for those who believe in the kind of power I have described to you. It will not go well for those who generate fear and hatred, it will not go well for those who believe in fear and hatred. For hell and damnation is what awaits those who have not accepted the gift that God has freely offered."

When Gene finished, Aaron looked at him. He had tears trickling down his cheeks. Aaron reached his hand up to his face and found, to his surprise, tears there as well. Aaron knew he was a Christian now. He knew that God had changed him. He just did not expect this much change this soon. Only a day ago, Aaron had been one of those people that was full of hatred and fear. Only a day ago, all his being was about accumulating the money and power that Gene had been preaching about. Only a day ago, he had been one of the ones headed for eternal hell and damnation. Only a day ago, he had sought to persecute, hunt, and even kill Christians. Now all the hate and fear were gone. He sought not to hurt people now; he sought to help them, protect them, and show them God's love. In one day, he had gone from Satan's ally to born again, redeemed, child of the most High God. He also knew that this gift was meant to be shared.

Aaron stopped in his tracks, dropped to his knees, and began to pray. The other three men when they saw Aaron, stopped, placed their hands on his shoulders, and prayed with him. There was no doubt that God was calling Aaron to bring others to Christ. He did not know how, where, or any who, but he did know that his prayer was that he listen to God, trust in God, and obey God.

After his Amen, Aaron rose, and the four of them began walking again. They walked in silence for some time. Aaron had been lost in his thoughts and for the longest time had not noticed that the tunnel had begun to slant upward. The tunnel walls were smoother, and there were Bible verses that were painted onto the walls. Some were written in their entirety, and others were just the book, chapter, and verse. It was like walking through a keelage of the Bible.

Aaron's fingers ran across the smooth wall. Some of the verses he had heard before, and he cherished those because he knew some of what they meant. The others he saw, he cherished because he didn't know, but it was the word of the living God, and he got to learn it.

Gene saw his reaction and said to him, "Just wait."

The tunnel opened into a huge cavern. The diameter had to be at least two hundred feet, the ceiling was seventy feet at its apex, and the majority of the cavern's surfaces were covered in Bible verses. Aaron stood at the entrance in a state of shock. Just as the tunnel leading here had been the entirety of the cave was covered in God's word. As his eyes took this wonder in, he noticed that there were people still writing and painting on the walls, floors, and even the ceiling of the cave.

Gene gave Aaron a gentle shove. "I told you hadn't seen anything yet. Welcome to the Word cave."

Aaron looked around still in awe of what he saw. "Uncle," he said, "is this where the Christian community hides?"

Gene smiled, grabbed Aaron's arm, and pulled him into the cave. "No, my friend, this is a way station of sorts. Here we can get some rest and food for our physical as well as the spiritual selves." The last he emphasized with a wave of his arm around the cavern.

Aaron nodded his head slowly in astonishment. The old man had a flair for understatement. They sat down and were brought some food and drink.

"When will we go to the main community?" Aaron asked as he shoved a large piece of bread into his mouth. He had not realized how hungry he had been.

His three traveling companions laughed at him. When Uncle Gene recovered, he said, "Soon, but God has other plans for us. For now, eat and rest, tomorrow has its own set of problems."

Aaron continued to shove food in his mouth, but his eyes never left the words printed on the cavern. He wanted to consume those words as he was consuming the bread he now held. He hungered for them. He must learn as much as possible, as soon as possible. After he finished eating, he rose to go read, but Gene laid a hand on his shoulder and simply said rest. He sat back down, and before he even knew he had, Aaron was fast asleep, surrounded, and hugged by the word of God.

# CHAPTER 24

## *The Bait*

Sloan's mood had gone from one of elation at the thought of torturing Aaron to one of rage at not being able to find the two men. *I mean one was well known in this side of town, and the other was an old man. How hard can it be to find the two of them?* Sloan thought.

The only way that they could have eluded the dragnet that he had put out into the city was if the people known as Christians were helping them. Of course, Christians, these days hid themselves very well. If they did not, it meant imprisonment at best or more likely torture and death.

It was time that Sloan took off the kid gloves. Aaron was not around any longer. Sloan was in charge of the group now. He would start just outside the marketplace and use his people to squeeze the information he needed out of the population. Sloan had never cared if people got hurt, but he had used restraint, just to keep a low profile—that is until now.

He turned to the two men following him. "Bring everyone and tell them to arm themselves. These people will tell us where our prey has gone to, or they will regret it."

The two men exchanged glances, questioning the wisdom of what they were hearing.

That is until Sloan drew the 9mm pistol and pointed it at them. "Go!"

Both men scrambled away and ran with the message of doom that they carried.

Sloan walked slowly down the street. "Bring me Aaron and the one called Uncle Gene!" he shouted. "Bring them to me or suffer!"

The few people that were out at this time of night; people tended to be off the streets early if they could, gazed upon a man devoid of compassion, and if they had any doubt, it was squashed when Sloan pulled the trigger on the gun and a man standing near a cross street fell as the bullet entered his chest.

Sloan shouted again, "Bring me Aaron and the one called Uncle Gene or suffer!"

Within an hour, almost every one of the populations of Sloan's army had gathered at the center of the marketplace. This was a logical place to begin the search. It was central to much of the city. From here, Sloan knew he could send out his troops and have a better chance of catching the two men.

Sloan stood atop one of the tables used for displaying goods. He still held the pistol in his hand, and he waved it around as he spoke.

"In groups of three or four, fan out from this location. Bring me Aaron and Gene. You bring them to me, and we will be rich. We will no longer have to scrounge a pitiful existence. Aaron has betrayed us, and Gene is a wanted Christian leader whom our government will pay handsomely for. Bring them to me alive. The two have information that will increase the payout. Oh, if any of you have thoughts of just taking them in yourselves, there is no place that you can hide that I will not find you, now go."

There was some milling about as the hundred or so people there divided into groups. Sloan grabbed a big grubby-looking man by the shoulder. The man spun around, not appreciating be pawed at. The face was large and weather-beaten. His hair was dirt brown, long a scraggly, and his beard looked as if it had never been trimmed. His eyes were angry gray, and he snarled at Sloan as he turned.

"I have a job for you."

"Get your hand off me," the man snarled as he raised his massive hand to slap Sloan.

At first, Sloan was frightened. He flinched back from the man. However, when the man raised his hand to strike Sloan, Sloan pulled his pistol and held it just under the man's nose.

"It's up to you, big man. Do you think you can swing that massive paw before I pull this trigger?"

The mountain of a man lowered his arm slowly. Sloan held the pistol in place for another beat and then lowered it and put it away.

"Good choice. What's your name?"

The voice that answered was deep and resonant, but it was also thoughtful. If you were unable to see him, you would swear you were speaking with a scholar.

"My name is Gregory Brendon, but everyone calls me Mongo after some movie character that was as big as I am."

"Well, Gregory, I need you to take this card, go to the government annex building, speak with a man there named, Rogan, give him this card, and he will know to come and help round up these vermin."

Sloan looked around. "I will be in that house there." Sloan pointed. "Bring him here when he arrives. Tell him to have his men be as loud and obnoxious about arresting these Christians as they can. Can you remember all that Mongo," Sloan added with a sarcastic grin.

After about five minutes, the only one left in the square was Sloan.

Sloan walked over to the door of the house he had pointed out to Gregory, raised his leg, and kicked at the door and the fragile thing exploded inward. Cowering in the corner were a man and his two daughters. The man rushed Sloan, and Sloan swung the pistol as a club. There was a dull thud, and the man went down in a heap.

Sloan sat down at the table in the middle of the room and smiled.

"Now, ladies, bring me food and drink, and we will get to know each other. I have questions, and I hope you have answers."

One of the women, a girl about eighteen years of age, got up and walked over to where her father lay. Delicate fingers checked for a pulse. The pretty face's tension dissolved as she discovered her father was still alive.

She then turned back to her sister. The sister was about thirteen years old. She had the same pretty features as her older sibling, but instead of the blond hair and blue eyes of the older sister, this one had brown hair and green eyes.

The eighteen-year-old helped her younger sister up. "Fran, go get this man some food and drink. Bring him some of the stew we have left and bring him the bottle of wine."

Her voice was strong, yet melodic like the ringing of a bell.

Fran nodded and left to follow her sister's instructions.

Sloan had been watching carefully. If they intended to do any harm to him, they would not catch him by surprise. Yet as the older of the two gave instructions and then turned to face him, there was not one hint of deception or subterfuge.

Sloan smiled as he sat down at the dining room table. This was a simple home. Ramshackle would be the best word Sloan could use to describe it. The front of the house consisted of a combination of a living room, dining room table, and a kitchen. The kitchen was separated by a waist-high wall, which did very little to give the illusion of a bigger place. There was a hallway that led off to the right, and Sloan assumed that bedrooms for the occupants must lie in that direction.

Impressions of lumber could be seen through the bare spots in the drywall while gaping holes showed entire sections of the wood that lay behind the walls. The lumber appeared to be solid. What little paint remained on the walls was one of those light baby blue colors. The color was meant to soothe, but all it did for Sloan was irritate him.

"You seem to be wise beyond your years, girl. What is your name?"

The eighteen-year-old squared her shoulders and said, "Rebecca." She stood still, but her eyes darted back and forth looking for any way that her sister and she could gain the upper hand.

With an evil grin, Sloan laid the gun on the table in front of him and tapped his long index finger on it.

"Now, Rebecca, so far the only person who has been hurt has been your father. Do not give me any other reasons to hurt him or either of you. All I want is nourishment and a few answers to my questions, and then you and your family can go back to your lives. Do we understand one another?"

Rebecca nodded and sat down across from Sloan, as Fran brought a steaming bowl of stew and bottle of wine and sat it down on the table. She then went and hid behind her sister Rebecca.

Sloan leaned down and drew in a huge breath. He sighed and said, "Now that smells delicious."

He picked up the spoon and began to gently put the hot contents in his mouth. He then took a drink of wine. "The stew is delicious, although I must admit the wine is too sweet for my taste.

Sloan could see the flinch of anger that crossed Rebecca's face, but she restrained herself from doing anything. Probably to protect her unconscious father and her frightened little sister.

The girl was brave, but she was smart as well. Sloan took his time finishing his meal and relished every twitch and flinch of anger he happened to see flash across Rebecca's face. Once he had slurped the last of the stew and drained the bottle of wine, he sat back, patted his stomach, and belched.

"Now that I have been fed, we can get down to the business at hand. I am looking for two men. One is a young man who goes by the name of Aaron. The other is an older man and goes by the name Uncle Gene."

Fran had been hiding behind her sister the whole time hardly making a peep. So when her breath caught, it was like a gun going off.

"Ah," Sloan said as he pushed the chair back slowly. He got up and walked to the end of the table, just so he could see Fran hiding behind her sister.

"I see you have at least heard of this man. Tell me where they are or where they might be hiding, and you will come through this unharmed."

Rebecca seemed lost in thought, and then she responded. "You seek both men harm. I will not help you harm another."

Sloan stepped closer to both girls. "Even if it will prevent harm from coming to you, your father, or lovely little sister? I know some people that would give me a lot of money for her."

Rebecca's face fell, and tears trickled out of the corner of her eyes, but she squared her shoulders and struck like a lioness protecting her cub, swiftly and without warning. She flung herself across the end of the table. Unfortunately for her, this was not the first time Sloan had threatened people, and he was ready for her reaction. He sidestepped her attack, gave her a little love tap with the butt of the pistol, and watched as she crashed to the ground.

In one quick stride, Sloan had Fran in his grasp. He used her hair as leverage and pulled her back into him. He leaned down and said, "Maybe I just keep you for myself," the leer of lust he directed at Rebecca. She had rolled into a sitting position and was trying to figure out how to get Fran out of Sloan's grasp.

Sloan smiled. "All you have to do is tell me where I can find Gene and Aaron, and this will all be over."

Sloan shoved Fran hard toward Rebecca. Both women went down in a heap on the floor. He kept the gun trained on them as he searched. He found some rope and cloth. This will do, he thought. He went over to the girl's father, tied him up, and stuffed enough cloth in his mouth that the man would not be able to talk. Sloan figured the father would be waking up soon, and he needed the man helpless to save his daughters.

He waved the gun at both daughters to indicate that they should sit down at the table.

He tied Fran's hands behind her back and gagged her mouth as well.

He left Rebecca just sitting there. He was not going to bind or gag her. He needed her to talk. He needed the location of Gene's hiding place. He needed…a thought occurred to him. Even if he got the information he sought, it may take him too long to get there. The two men may get away or be warned. He would get them to come to him.

Oh, this was pure genius. Sloan always knew he was smarter than everyone else. Now he would prove it.

Sloan walked over to Fran and put the gun against her temple. Fran let out a cry. Rebecca tensed but did not move.

Sloan's smile became a thing of satisfaction and pure evil.

"New plan, I do not need you to tell me where they are. I just need you to wait with me. Soon, they will come to me."

Rebecca bowed her head and prayed. "Father, provide for and protect us. Father, put Your protection around Uncle Gene and this Aaron person. Father, please forgive this man, and may he come to know Your love through our Lord and Savior, Christ Jesus."

As Sloan heard her praying for him, he became livid. In two strides, he stood in front of her. "I don't need your forgiveness and, I don't need the lies of this Christ!" he screamed, spittle flying from his lips and splashing Rebecca's face. Sloan pointed the gun at her forehead. His finger tightened on the trigger. He tried to shoot her in the face, but his finger would not move any further. Sweat poured down his face from the strain until he relented.

He lowered the gun. "You live for now, girl, sit there and don't speak."

Rebecca obeyed and sat down. She knew that God had sent His angels to protect her. "Thank You, Lord."

# CHAPTER 25

## *No Choice*

Aaron bolted and sat up so fast his head spun. As his eyes focused, he saw Uncle Gene standing above him and shaking his arm.

Gene smiled, as Aaron got to his feet. "Man, you were gone. I take it you slept well?"

Aaron rubbed his eyes and stretched. "Better than I have slept in years."

"Having the peace of God definitely helps you sleep better." Gene chuckled. "The Holy Spirit beats a glass of warm milk any day."

Aaron paused, walking with Gene for a moment and looked at the old man.

"What?" Gene asked.

"You just are not what I expected a Christian to be. You make jokes about the Holy Spirit, you do not judge, and you show everyone respect and compassion. I thought Christians were supposed to be more serious. I thought they we supposed to be more fire and brimstone and less Laurel and Hardy."

Gene patted Aaron on the back and bade him to continue walking. Aaron could smell bacon cooking somewhere in the cave, and his stomach informed him that it was definitely time to eat.

"Aaron, don't you realize that God has a sense of humor? God created all of us. We are reflections of Him until through our choices we separate ourselves from Him. When we accept Christ as our

Savior, we are reunited and reconciled with God. Our joy, our peace, and yes, even our humor is guided by His holy spirit. Christians are not doom and gloom, we are the life of the party."

Aaron started laughing, and Gene joined him. The two men were still laughing as they sat down near the fire, and Tiny handed both a plate that was filled with eggs and bacon.

Tiny snorted and looked at Uncle Gene. "You told him the Holy Spirit warm milk joke didn't you."

Gene smiled. "You know me so well, Sam."

Sam cringed and gave Uncle Gene a frowning look. "I am sorry, my friend, you know me so well, Tiny."

Aaron laughed and said, "You prefer your nickname to your real name?"

Tiny sat down and began to eat his breakfast. "I find it fits better than Sam."

"You know, we could call you Tiny Sam or TS for short, then you could be known as T. S. Elliot," Aaron said and waited.

There was a short pause of shock, then all three men busted out laughing.

Uncle Gene wiped a tear of joy from his eye and stated, "You see, Christians are the life of the party.

The sound of rapidly pounding feet cut into their revery. The three men stood and faced one of the adjoining tunnels. They put their plates down and prepared to hide or fight. It was then that they saw an out-of-breath Fergus come sprinting into the cave. He ran up to Uncle Gene and tried to speak, but all that came out were panicked gasps.

Gene gave Fergus a canteen. "Take a drink of water and calm yourself."

Fergus grabbed the canteen and took a long pull from it. He gave the canteen to Aaron and bent over at the waist with his hands on his knees. After a few minutes of long shuddering breaths, Fergus stood upright and the look on his face was ashen.

Gene frowned, his brow crinkled and the look of anguish on his face made him look twenty years older than he was. "What is it, Fergus? Just tell us."

A sob broke from Fergus's lips, and then all he had to report came out in a rush.

"Uncle Gene, the government is moving on the marketplace and all the housing in the area. They are brutalizing people, and they are arresting any who they identify as a Christian or Christian sympathizer. They are rounding everyone up. They are using a PA system to announce that unless you and Aaron give yourselves up, or those in the area give them your location they will kill or imprison everyone. What do we do, Uncle Gene? What do we do?"

Gene sighed, bowed his head, and prayed. Silently, he said, "Oh Lord, how long? Please protect all of those in danger. What is Your will, oh God, send me where You will." Gene lifted his head and saw all three men looking at him with anxious anticipation.

Aaron was amazed at the look of peace on the old man's face, and when he spoke, it was clear that God spoke through him.

Gene looked at Fergus. "Calm yourself, Fergus, and remember who you serve. In Proverbs 3:5, God tells us, 'Trust in the Lord with all your heart and lean not on your own understanding.' We, of course, will be about the Father's work."

Fergus took a deep breath and was calmer now. "Yes, Uncle, forgive me for my panic."

Gene patted him on the shoulder and said, "There is nothing to forgive, this is troubling news, but God is with us, and His provision and protection surround us. Now, Fergus, you and Tiny go to the community and let them know what is happening. Tell them all to pray and be ready."

Tiny turned and drew himself up to his tallest and said, "No, I will go with you, Uncle. I will not let you go into danger and not be there to protect you."

Uncle Gene, seeing and hearing Tiny's defiant stance and tone, used his no-nonsense disciplinary voice.

"Tiny, I do not need your protection, I appreciate your loyalty, but I have told you where God wants you. I have my road to walk with my Lord, and you have yours. Now go and do as I say."

Tiny lowered his head and said in a much lower volume, "Yes, sir."

Tiny sounded like a chastised child, a child who was ashamed of questioning the elder.

Aaron was astounded at the power in Gene's voice. That tone, that sound, brokered no defiance. It was power itself. Aaron realized that if Gene wanted, he could command armies. Then Aaron realized that Gene did command an army, just one that was not bent on destruction and violence.

Gene turned to Aaron, "You and I must go. We will be putting ourselves in the mouth of the lion, but like Daniel, the Lord God is with us."

"I understand, let us be about the work of the Lord."

Aaron put his arms around the men he called brothers now. They joined in a loose circle, and without a word, they all bowed their heads, and Aaron began to pray.

"Lord God, we do not know what is going to happen, but we know that we trust You. We know that evil men hold our friends and neighbors, but we also know that You are the one in control, not them. Lord, give us the wisdom to know Your will and the strength to do Your will. Protect my brothers, Fergus and Tiny, as they go to prepare the others. Lord, bring Uncle Gene and me to wherever we can do the best for those in danger. Your will be done Lord, in Jesus's name I pray. Amen."

The three others replied, "Amen."

The group shared one last look at each other and then went their separate ways.

"What is the fastest route to the market from here?" Aaron voiced the question as he looked around the cave, there were several branches off this main cave, and he was really lost at this point.

Gene pointed to the right and said, "This way."

Uncle Gene walked toward the exit with Aaron. He saw a flash of worry and dread cross Aaron's face. "Trust not in your own understanding, trust in the Lord. So be of great joy, we go to do the Father's will," he said as they walked out of the cave.

# CHAPTER 26

## Satan's Army

Rogan Blass hated being called out of his office, and he especially hated being called out into this festering part of the city. But as he was the one put in charge of rooting out the seditious faction known as Christians and his informant Sloan had called for reinforcements, he had no choice but to back the play and try to bring as many of the scum to justice as possible. Plus, if he could bring in the one known as Uncle Gene, his upper trajectory would be assured. Then he would really find his star rising.

"After all," he whispered as he walked out the door of his office, "nothing gets you promoted faster than bringing in Christians."

Rogan stood under an arch that served as a sign of the marketplace he was about to enter. Behind him stood thirty-five fully armored and armed special agents. These guys were no joke. Dressed in black Kevlar armor, armed with submachine guns, pistols, stun grenades, and stun batons, they were equipped to take subversives dead or alive.

Rogan had the privilege of supervising these people, and he knew they were committed to ridding the planet of Christians. *These so-called saved people. They thought themselves better than everyone else. They thought they were saved by God. How arrogant*, Rogan thought. There was no place for God in this society. After all, they were not primitives looking for a reason why things happened. People had long ago outgrown God. They were intellectuals; they knew how the world worked and how the universe worked.

They were accepting of all people, no matter what they really thought of them, everyone except these Christians. Rogan and this regime did not accept them because they had the audacity to tell people that they were sinners, that they were wrong in their choices. Everyone knew that there was no such thing as wrong and right. The fact that Christians defied the government law that there is no God, except humans themselves, gave Rogan and his troops all the justification they needed to round them up and even kill them if they resisted.

One of his men ran up to Rogan. "Sir," he said as he saluted, "we've located your informant. He is two streets over in one of what passes for a house in this area."

Rogan returned the salute and gave a man a sly smile. "Lead the way, Sergeant."

The man saluted again. "Yes, sir." He moved off in the direction he had indicated.

"The rest of you, move out, find every Christian outlaw in this area. If they resist, subdue them and bring them in for questioning. If they still resist, kill them." Rogan really hoped a lot of them resisted. The faster they rid themselves of these vermin the better. Rogan Blass' grey eyes flashed with glee as he barked the order.

He snapped his head toward the sergeant and moved after him quickly so he could catch up.

The sergeant opened the door, and Rogan walked in. The place was a hovel of a house with only two rooms that could be called rooms. The rest was partitioned off with curtains for privacy, he supposed. While the place was a dump, Rogan had to admit that it was kept cleaner than his apartment.

"Well, well, well, you always take me to the nicest places, Sloan," he said in irritation as he walked over and sat down across from Sloan at the table.

Sloan drained the glass of water he had been drinking and slammed the glass down on the table. His shoulders leaned toward

Rogan, his eyes widened in anger as he spat out, "You took your sweet time, Rogan."

The sergeant took a step forward at what he perceived as a challenge to his boss. Rogan held up his chunky hand. The sergeant stopped in his tracks.

"Now, now, we are all friends here. Sloan is just anxious to capture the outlaw, Gene. This is why we are here, isn't it, Sloan?"

Some of the tension left Sloan's body. "You know it is. I wouldn't have called you out otherwise. It is this waiting; it has got me on edge is all."

Rogan slowly pulled on the fingers of his black gloves as he removed them. He said, "I understand it is a tense situation. I see that you had a meal with these fine Christian folk as you waited. Some might say that sharing a meal with them is an act of sedition. I wouldn't, of course, but the sergeant there might think that you can't be trusted." The last word was emphasized with Rogan laying his gloves down on the table.

Sloan's lips tightened. "I confiscated a meal from them. I did not share a meal with them. Rogan, you're a slimy bag of blubber."

Rogan put his right hand on his chest and mocked being injured. "Ouch, stop it! You'll hurt my feelings."

Rogan showing utter disdain for Sloan turned to address the sergeant, "What do you think, Sergeant? Should I trust him? Especially since he said such hurtful things to me?"

The sergeant stepped up to where he was standing behind and just to the right of Rogan, making it clear that he had his commander's back. "It is your call, sir. I wouldn't, but your call. Say the word, and I will end him for you." The sergeant tapped the submachine gun he held in his hands and smiled at Sloan.

Rogan turned back to Sloan as he said, "Why thank you, Sergeant. It is good to know you have my back."

Rogan's face grew dark, the façade of civility left it all together. "You see how easy it would be to end your miserable life, Sloan? Listen and understand because I will only say this once. You're not in control here. If Gene is foolish enough to show up, then he is my prisoner. You will get whatever I decide to give you. Is that clear?"

Each word of the question was emphasized with a slap of Rogan's hand on the table.

Sloan wanted nothing more than to kill both idiots, but he needed Rogan and his men at this point to pull this off, so he swallowed the bile rising in his throat and responded with, "Perfectly."

"Ah, good," Rogan purred.

He pointed at the girl standing in terror in what passed for a kitchen. "You girl, bring me and the sergeant whatever you fed Sloan here and don't dilly or dally."

The girl nodded and started to prepare a bowl of stew for Rogan.

Rebecca sat two bowls of stew down on the table. They would go hungry tonight. She could not help herself; she chuckled as she moved away. She did so because going hungry seemed such a silly thought. They may now survive this.

Rogan heard the chuckle and turned his attention in full to the girl. "You find something amusing my dear?" His voice was dripping sweet as he asked the question.

Rebecca froze. She did not want to look at this man, but she knew she must give him an answer. She slowly turned back toward him. "No, sir, I'm just afraid."

Rogan patted the bench. "Oh, come now, come sit next to me. I will protect you."

Rebecca froze again. Every part of her wanted to run.

Rogan's eyes grew cold. "I said sit, my dear." There was nothing inviting in his tone, it was a command. "Perhaps your sister would prefer to sit next to me," Rogan added as he turned his attention to Rebecca's little sister.

Rebecca moved instantly and sat down next to Rogan. "No, sir, I will sit with you."

Rogan smiled and patted her on her leg as she sat. "Excellent, I can see we will get along just fine. Maybe after all this unpleasantness is over, you can come and visit me. I can take real good care of you."

Rebecca cringed at his touch and his words. *Please, Lord, save us*, she prayed silently.

Rogan and the sergeant finished their meal. Once Rogan saw the sergeant was done, he barked his orders to him. "Sergeant, go out and organize the men. When the rebel Gene shows up, make sure he is brought here. Understood?"

The sergeant snapped to attention, saluted, and shouted, "Yes, sir."

Rogan held up a finger. "And, Sergeant, you don't have to be too gentle with him, but make sure he is in good enough shape to answer questions."

"Yes, sir, indeed, sir."

The sergeant left, and Rogan stared at Sloan. Rogan rubbed his hands together briskly and with a glee of anticipation and dug into the stew with gusto. Around bites, he said, "Now we wait."

# CHAPTER 27

## *Delivered*

As Aaron and Gene walked down the street, people either moved aside to the sidewalk to allow them to pass, or they placed themselves in front of them. Aaron glanced at Uncle Gene, a question in his mind.

Gene smiled. "The ones that are going in front of us are believers. To their credit, they seek to protect us from the bad people ahead. It is their way of supporting us. They will not be able to protect us for long. What is to come must be faced by you and me, but it is good to see nonetheless."

They continued to walk, and within two blocks of where they knew they were heading, a crowd of perhaps two hundred surrounded them. To Aaron, it was as if they had a human shield going before them. Even the black-suited, jack-booted government goons were keeping their distance. Aaron could not tell if it was because they were afraid or if they simply did not know who was in the center of the mass of humanity. Aaron suspected it was the latter.

Many of the people who were nearest to Gene were thanking him touching him, and more than once, Aaron heard praise Jesus, praise God. Aaron could not help but be filled with joy, his face hurt from smiling. To see so many walking with them filled his heart. Several times he felt one in the crowd pat him on the shoulder or back and say, "Thank you, brother."

They were moving so rapidly, and there were so many around them that Aaron had no way to acknowledge all of them. He didn't know what he had expected, but it was not this.

At some point, the crowd began to sing. Aaron did not know the song, but he could have sworn he heard Onward Christian Soldiers as some of the words. The singing came to an abrupt halt as the unmistakable boom of a pistol thundered out into the air. People instinctively ducked or dove for cover.

Aaron was searching for a place to bolt to and take cover when Gene placed his hand on his shoulder. Aaron looked up and saw Gene's eyes were glacial. Gene shook his head, and Aaron stood back up.

The crowd parted. Standing in the road in front of them was the biggest government goon Aaron had ever seen. He wore sergeant's strips, and he held a 9mm pistol in his right hand, pointed toward the open sky. This had been the source of the gunshot.

The big man lowered the gun and pointed it first at Gene, then at Aaron, and then waved it toward the crowd as he spoke.

"You all have one minute to vacate this area before my men, and I help you on your way." He pointed the pistol in the air again and squeezed off another round. Without the buffer of the crowd around them, this shot was loud enough to make Aaron's ears ring.

The crowd reacted; they began to scramble in all directions. Thirty seconds later the only ones left in the street were the big sergeant, five of what Aaron assumed were his men, Gene, himself, and most of the Christian brothers and sisters that had walked with them. They had backed off some, but they were still there.

Aaron looked around, and all of them were silently praying or watching Uncle Gene for the word to attack.

Aaron heard the sergeant chuckle, and his men joined in. The sergeant then pointed at Gene and asked, "Seems like all of you have a death wish. Well, I am happy to oblige, boys."

The sergeants' men tightened a group around him. They're machine pistols held at the ready.

Tense murmurs rippled through the crowd, and Aaron heard an increase in volume from those who were praying.

Gene stepped closer to the sergeant and whispered to him.

"Do you really think your boss inside is going to appreciate all the paperwork you're about to generate for him? These people have not threatened you, and they have done nothing to you or you men. If you shoot them, your boss is going to be very cross with you. I am the one that he is looking for. Just take me to him, and all this can be avoided."

The sergeant nodded. "Tell your servants to go home."

Gene looked at the sergeant. "Oh, they are not my servants. They serve one far greater than I, but I will speak to them."

Gene turned to the crowd when he spoke his voice was calm, but it carried over the paved street like a wave of thunder.

"My friends, we must speak to some people inside. Stay, if you will, and pray. Thank you so much for your support and bravery. I thank God for you every day. Now let us go in peace."

The tension in the crowd evaporated. All of them began to pray.

Gene turned back to the sergeant, patted Aaron on the shoulder, and said, "This is Aaron. He is with me. Where I go, he goes."

The sergeant said, "I was told to only admit you. My boss is waiting for you. He waits out here with us."

Gene walked up to the big man holding the gun, placed his hand on the weapon, and with a gentle push, lowered the weapon as he said, "No, as I said, where I go, he goes."

The sergeant's face was one of stunned disbelief. He opened his mouth to protest, and he tried to raise the gun, but neither one of those things happened. Instead, Gene turned and waved to Aaron, "Come, my brother, let us be about God's work this day."

As Aaron walked toward Gene, he looked up, and standing in the doorway to a small home was a man he had only met once. Rogan, Aaron remembered his name, but moreover, Aaron knew his reputation as a ruthless bureaucrat who had made his way up the ranks by hunting down Christians. Aaron had seen God do miraculous things, but despite all of that, Aaron swallowed hard. He did not see a way that he and Gene survived walking into this home.

As if Gene had read Aaron's mind, he whispered, "Greater is He that is in us than he that is in this world."

Aaron squared his shoulders, and both men walked through the doorway.

The scene that greeted them was one of despair and sadness. A man lay in the corner, dead. Two girls sat at the table, their heads lowered in what Aaron assumed was either prayer, grief, or both.

Rogan smiled, and his voice dripped evil as he welcomed them. "Well, the famous, or should I say infamous, Uncle Gene, and color me surprised a bonus guest, Aaron, right? Oh, I have someone here who is going to be most pleased to see you again. Please sit, gentlemen."

Gene and Aaron walked to the table and sat down on the bench seats across from the two young girls. Just as Aaron got seated, stepping out of the shadows of what Aaron presumed was the home's kitchen, he saw Sloan.

Sloan's face was a mixture of satisfaction and rage, as he raised his own pistol level with Aaron's head.

Sloan's hand shook with the need to pull the trigger. Just an ounce more pressure and Aaron would be no more.

"Now, now, Sloan, we have business with these gentlemen. Lower your weapon. If they do not give us what we want, then you can shoot him multiple times then blow his head off."

Sloan didn't lower the gun. Rogan's voice snapped, the heat of his anger seeping through. "Remember our deal, Sloan. If you pull that trigger now, you get nothing."

Sloan hesitated for just a moment longer, then lowered his weapon. "Fine," he said through clenched teeth, "but you remember, he is mine when we're done."

Rogan walked over to the other side of the table and sat down next to the older of the two girls. He placed an arm around her and began speaking as if they were all old friends.

"Well, Gene, may I call you Gene?" Rogan said, as he tightened his grip on the girl and laid his pistol in front of him on the table. She visibly cringed. Aaron tensed, as he leaned forward. Even before he was a Christian, Aaron hated child abusers. Gene laid a gentle arm on his shoulder and Aaron relaxed.

Gene then turned his attention to Rogan. "You may call me Gene. It is my name after all."

Rogan's smile slipped for a moment. The calm in the man's voice unnerved him a bit, this guy should at least be a little nervous, then he continued, "Excellent, so we all are on the same page, let us review what is on the agenda. I have called you here so you can do the right thing and help us bring all those seditious followers of yours to justice. To that end, if you will just give us their location, then we can wrap this up early, and I can be home by dinner time. So where are they?"

Rogan emphasized the question as he tapped his pistol on the table.

Aaron had always thought of Rogan as just a greasy bureaucrat, but the guy was handling this situation as if he were a manager in a business meeting, and he really needed to get his hands off the girl.

*Please, God,* Aaron silently prayed, *just let me punch this guy in the face.*

Gene shook his head, and his ice-blue eyes gazed at Rogan. Gene then ignored Rogan and turned his attention to the girl. "What is your name child?"

"Rebecca, sir."

Gene reached out his hand in greeting and said, "Nice to meet you, Rebecca. I am Gene."

Rebecca began to take Gene's extended hand, but Rogan caught her hand and slammed it down on the table. Rebecca let out a small cry of pain and shrunk back, but she did acknowledge Gene.

"I know, sir, you are Uncle Gene. All the brothers and sisters know who you are."

Rogan backhanded Rebecca off the seat. She landed with a thud and blood welled on her lip. "How touching, but it hardly furthers our goals. Where are your lawbreakers hiding, Gene?"

Aaron shot across the table and was able to get his hands on Rogan, but the barrel of the pistol left a circular impression on his forehead it was pressed in so hard. Aaron let go of Rogan and inched his way back across the table, but he did not sit back down.

Gene got up and walked around the table, ignoring Rogan. He leaned down and picked Rebecca up off the floor. He patted her cheek once she was on her feet. "Rebecca, do you and your sister know the Lord?"

Rebecca's response was one of instantaneous joy. "Oh yes, sir, we know Jesus as our Lord and Savior, thank you for asking."

Rogan had stood as Gene had made his way over to the girl. When he spoke, his voice cracked a little with anger. His control was slipping. "Gene, I did not bring you here to recruit others to their doom. I brought…"

Gene cut Rogan off, "You didn't bring me here. My God brought me here."

Gene hugged the child as a father would his daughter. "Well then, my sister in Christ, you know that these men have no power over us," he whispered to her. "Go into the kitchen, tend your wound, and watch out after your sister. Can you do that for me?"

"Yes, sir," Rebecca said as she turned to go.

Gene smiled as he heard her humming, "Amazing Grace."

Gene turned standing there was him was Rogan. "There seems to be some misunderstanding, let me clear that up right now. If you do not tell me what I want to know, I am going to kill all of you. You're all confessed Christians. No one will miss you. I would be as celebrated as a doctor who removed a cancerous tumor, especially for cutting you out Gene." Rogan spat the words Christian and Gene's name as if he had tasted something sour.

For the first time since entering the home, Gene turned his complete attention to Rogan. Gene smiled. "There does seem to be a misunderstanding here. You are operating under the assumption that you have control here, you do not. God brought us here so that His will could be accomplished. There is a purpose to His will. I pray that His will is that you be saved by our Lord and Savior, Christ Jesus."

Rogan laughed and began to pace around the room. "So God has brought you here? God wants you to be tortured. God wants the hiding place of your so-called flock to be revealed. Because that is what is happening here, nothing else. Now tell me what I want to know."

Gene arched his eyebrow and shook his head again in sympathy. "God's will is that none should be lost. His will is that all would be saved. His love for us is infinite, and even now He is trying to save you, Rogan. God has tried many times to reach you, and every time you have rejected God."

A flash of anger and hatred sparked on Rogan's face. His hand clenched on the pistol. "I do not know what you're talking about. God has never reached out to me. I think you are trying to provoke me into killing you before I get what I want but no, old man. You will tell me where your vermin are hiding."

Uncle Gene looked Rogan squarely in his eyes, and even though Rogan held the gun, even though he appeared to be the one in control when Gene spoke it was as if a father was speaking to a rude and disobedient child. "You know very well, Rogan. You were raised in a home that believed. Your mother and father tried to teach you the ways of the Lord, but you rejected them. You have read the Bible, you know that when Jesus returns His judgment will be at hand, and all chances to accept God's love and forgiveness will be lost. Remember what you read. Look around you. These are the end times. Jesus's return is not far now. You are running out of chances."

Rogan raised the pistol in his right hand and pointed it at Gene's chest. "How do you know all of that, old man?" Rogan screamed.

Gene's voice was steady and calm in the face of the fear and hatred being thrown at him, and he replied, "I know because the Holy Spirit reveals what I need to know, to show God's love for you. This is your last chance. Will you accept God's love and accept Jesus as your Savior and Lord?"

Rogan lashed out and struck Gene with the pistol. The blow caught Gene on the forehead, and Gene went down. Gene sat up and blood poured from the wound. Aaron ran over to Gene and pulled him to his feet.

"Are you alright, Uncle?" Aaron asked.

Gene's legs were wobbly, and Aaron placed Gene's arm around his shoulder to support him.

Rogan backed away a few steps. Took some deep breaths to calm himself. He tried to go back to his even-keeled demeanor, but the facade had broken, and his fear and hatred of all things Christian continued to seep through.

"I think we are getting off course again, but just so there are no misconceptions here. I reject you, your God, and Jesus. I am a man of intellect, not hocus pocus superstition. I am here to bring your people to justice and that is what I will do. Do you understand me, old man?"

Gene stood on his own power now. Aaron stepped away as Gene moved closer to Rogan. "So be it. Your decision has been made. I am sorry."

Gene turned toward Sloan, and it was the first time he had even looked his way. "What about you, Sloan?"

The question was a simple one, but Sloan felt as if he had been belly-punched. All the air went out of his lungs. He just stared at Gene and Aaron. When he regained his composure, he asked in a small quiet voice, "Why would you ask me? I have pursued you. I have turned in Christians, I have done so many bad things to you and yours. Why would you ask me to accept your God? It must be evident to even you that I am with Rogan."

Gene smiled. "I am only the messenger. It is not *I* who is asking, it is God. He loves you and wants to save you."

Rogan strode over to Sloan. "Do not listen to that fool. All we need is the location of the camp, and we will have everything we want. You will have everything you want. We are close now, Sloan. Don't engage in this insanity."

Sloan looked at Rogan and nodded his head yes. Sloan then pointed his pistol at Gene, then Aaron. He alternated between the two men. "Tell us what we want to know."

Gene's gift from the Holy Spirit had always been an ability to read people, and he saw doubt in Sloan. Sloan had heard all that had been said, and Gene could tell that Sloan had questions. He also could tell that Sloan did not trust the promises coming from Rogan.

"Sloan, you still have a chance to be saved by our Lord and Savior, Jesus. No matter what you have done."

Sloan looked at Gene. The pistol shook in his hand. *How does this man know what I am thinking?* The gun lowered as Sloan's fear of Gene took hold.

Rogan slapped Sloan on the back of his head. "Wake up you idiot. The old man is trying to get in your head, he is trying to divide us. I'm warning you, Sloan. If you don't help me get the information, I will make sure you're put away with the rest of the trash."

Sloan whipped around and brought his gun to bear on Rogan. "Don't touch me!" he screamed.

Rogan was stunned by Sloan's reaction. He backed away, saying, "Okay, Sloan, don't do anything you'll regret. You shoot me, and you will spend the rest of your life in prison. Right now, we can still salvage this. You shoot me though, and neither of us gets what we want."

Sloan lowered his pistol, his other hand rubbed across his eyes. This was supposed to be an easy payday; he was supposed to be in the lap of luxury already. He never trusted Rogan, but now he did not think Rogan ever intended to live up to his part of their bargain.

As his hand came away from his face, he saw Rogan, pointing the gun at him.

"Well," Rogan said in his narcissistic condescending tone, "I believe it is time to end our little partnership. Such a shame, I was just going to frame you as being a Christian sympathizer, but I can see that you need to be put down as the mongrel you are."

Gene lunged. He knocked Sloan aside. Several things registered all at once. The retort of thunder in his ears from the gun, and a searing burning ripping pain in his gut. The scream of anguish from Aaron, and a struggle somewhere near him as he hit the floor hard. Gene faded in and out of consciousness as he lay there. So when he opened his eyes and saw Aaron holding both guns in his hands, he was really confused.

Blood pooled underneath Gene; this was not good. *Father, please heal me one more time, but not my will but Your will in Jesus's name. Amen.*

Gene heard Aaron hollering at him. "Uncle, Uncle, oh please, God, help him."

Gene saw Sloan. He was in shock, and he looked to see the man curled up in the corner. Clarity returned, it was Sloan he was here to save, and it was Sloan that God was revealing Himself to.

Gene rolled over on his side. Pain shot across his belly, but he ignored it. He reached out his hand to Sloan. "Sloan, come over here please."

Sloan's eyes shot back and forth; he looked like an animal that was trapped in a cage. At the sound of Gene's voice, he focused and uncurled. He just sat in the corner now. How was he in a corner cowering? What had just happened? As he saw Gene reaching out a hand to him, he had to know.

"Why would you sacrifice yourself for me?"

Gene grunted in pain as he responded, "For love, I could not let you die, knowing that you do not have the forgiveness of my Lord Jesus. I am already sealed. I know where I will go when I die. I had to give you the chance to be saved."

Gene grunted in pain again and coughed, which caused him to keen in pain.

Sloan looked at Gene with sadness and with wonder. "It is too late for me. You do not know the things I have done."

Gene struggled to breathe, but said, "It does not matter what you have done. The only thing that matters is the love of Christ, His mercy is sufficient, His grace is sufficient to save all of us. As far as it being too late, until Jesus our Lord and Savior returns you can still accept Him into your heart. You can still be saved. For those who seek Him they will find him. Seek the Lord, He loves you, He wants to save you, but you must accept His salvation. You must admit your sins, repent of them, and let go of your fear and hatred. Jesus loves you, Sloan, and He is not willing that any should perish in their sin. Seek Him with all your heart. Do not wait because when he returns it will be too late."

Sloan's confusion and anger were threatening to boil over. His eyes darted from Aaron to Rogan, and finally to the old man's eyes. Sloan could tell the old man was not afraid. Sloan saw resolve in those eyes; he saw peace.

Gene continued, "Sloan, you have been deceived your whole life. This man"—Gene darted his head toward the unconscious form of Rogan on the floor—"seeks to deceive you into hell. He knows that God is real, he rejected God long ago, but even so, if he asked God would forgive him, this is how much love God has for us. We could reject Him a million times and if we asked, He would forgive us and accept us. Do not let another deceive you, make up your own mind. Stop following the loudest voice in the room, that is what everyone else does. Instead, listen to the calm peaceful voice. That is God trying to get your attention. He is reaching out to you, but you must make the decision to receive His gift of salvation."

Gene grunted in pain again, the pool of blood underneath him was growing larger. Aaron leaned over him and asked, "What can I do, Uncle?"

Gene smiled at Aaron, and then he turned and looked at Sloan again. "Sloan, even after we are gone, God still loves you and is trying to save you. Listen to Him and accept His gift of salvation."

"Going?" Aaron asked. "We can't go anywhere. You are too hurt to be moved. I will go and get help after I tie these two up." Aaron waved the pistol in Rogan's general direction.

Gene smiled. "There is no need, yes, Lord, take us home."

Sloan had blinked his eyes. Before the blink, Aaron and Gene were there in front of him. After the blink, they were just gone.

He sat in the corner dumbfounded for several minutes. What had just happened? He had not passed out. He had just blinked. They did not walk away out of the door; they were just gone. He looked around finally and discovered that not only had Aaron and Gene vanished, but the two girls and their recently deceased father were no longer in the room either. This was impossible. People did not just vanish into thin air.

Sloan pushed himself up off the floor. He thought about killing Rogan; the man was still out, and it would be the prudent thing to do. After all, Rogan had tried to kill him. Then he remembered Gene's sacrifice and his words. Sloan had to get out of here. All he wanted was to not be here. Sloan heard Gene's voice over and over in his head. Seek the Lord and you will find Him.

# *EPILOGUE*

Seven weeks ago, Sloan had seen the impossible happen. He had seen four people disappear out of a room in the blink of an eye. It got much creepier than that though. He had walked out the door of the house and found the sergeant and his guards standing there in stunned disbelief. As he walked past the sergeant, the sergeant said in a fear-filled quiet tone.

"Where did they all go?"

It was then that Sloan realized that all the people who had been there supporting Gene had also vanished without a trace. The sergeant just kept repeating to himself, "Where did they all go?" The sergeant was losing it. *Like you're any different*, Sloan chuckled, and he felt what little sanity he had slipped away. *I must get out of here.* Sloan took off at a dead sprint. All he knew was that he could not be anywhere near here anymore.

Seven weeks ago, he had witnessed the impossible. After a few days of getting drunk and trying to numb the pain, he decided there must be a rational explanation, and he would find it. Sloan listened to the explanations being given by the government. They said that half the population of the planet was disintegrated by a new weapon, and other agencies reported that the Christian cult had found a way to destroy half the population, still others reported that it had been a massive alien abduction.

The truth was they had no idea what had happened. He had learned long ago that the government and the media stirred up fear and hatred to control the population. The story that was being pushed the most and the one that gaining momentum was that the

Christians were responsible for the disappearances. Sloan had to find out for himself why.

Seven weeks ago, he had witnessed the impossible. He went from place to place, spoke with person after person, and while there was no shortage of opinions about what had happened, he knew that he still did not know. His search took him to a library, he spent days in there rummaging through everything he could find, but still, the answer eluded him. He thought back to the day it had happened. Gene had said something right before that vanished. He had tried to remember before, but on this day in the quiet of the library, he remembered.

Aaron told Gene he had to go get help. Gene had said, "There is no need, yes, Lord, take us home." Sloan slumped in his chair. That was it; God had taken them. Sloan didn't want to believe that, but his need to find out why all those people had disappeared drove him to know, so he went and found a Bible. He spent the next week reading and searching through it trying to find out what had happened.

Seven weeks ago, he had seen the impossible, today he found out what had happened. Sloan found it, proof, that God had taken His people home. In 1 Corinthians 15:51–52, it reads, "Listen, I tell you a mystery: We will not all sleep, but we will be changed—in a flash, in the twinkling of an eye, at the last trumpet. For the trumpet will sound, the dead will be raised imperishable, and we will be changed."

Sloan also found a verse that explained why Gene had been willing to sacrifice himself. In the Bible, in the book of John 15:13, Jesus told His disciples, "Greater love has no one than this, that he lay down his life for his friends." This is what Gene had done for him. But more importantly, this is what the Christians say Jesus had done.

Sloan's mind raced; this was not possible. He had to find a more reasonable explanation. Man was enlightened now; Sloan did not believe in this mumbo-jumbo superstition. He just had to dig more, and he would find an explanation.

For three days after, Sloan read everything he could find on the end days. He searched for an explanation in almost every culture. As much as he tried to deny it, as much as he didn't want to know it, he could not refute that the end days that the Bible talks about were upon them. That the taking of all the Christians was the beginning of the last chapter in humanity's reign on this earth.

The verse that convinced him of it was 2 Timothy 3:1–5.

> But mark this: There will be terrible time in the last days. People will be lovers of themselves, lovers of money, boastful, proud, abusive, disobedient to their parents, ungrateful, unholy, without love, unforgiving, slanderous, without self-control, brutal, not lovers of the good, treacherous, rash, conceited, lovers of pleasure rather than lovers of God—having a form of godliness but denying its power. Have nothing to do with such people.

It was right there. The passage not only described him but also all the people who were left on this miserable planet. Sloan couldn't sluff this off a coincidence; he could no longer just ignore it. The vanishings, the description of the end days, it was all true.

Sloan shot out of the chair he had been sitting in and shoved it back so hard that it crashed to the floor behind him. With tears streaming out of his face, he shook his fists at the ceiling, at the heavens, at God, and in a guttural pain-filled sound that echoed throughout the mostly empty library screamed, "No! You cannot exist. If you are real, then we all have been lied to. I do not want this. I want to be ignorant again. This is too painful. Please, God." It was then that Sloan realized that he had been praying to a God that seven weeks ago, he had not believed in.

All strength left his legs, and he fell to his knees, then prone until his face was on the floor, and for the first time in his life, he prayed. "Father God, I know I am a sinner, I repent of my sins and ask that you forgive me. I know that you gave your only begotten son, Jesus Christ, to save me and all who call on his name. Please,

Lord Jesus, save me, I cannot and will not deny you any longer. In Jesus's name, I pray. Amen."

For what seemed like an eternity but was only a few moments, Sloan stayed prone and sobbed. His heart was broken, his mind filled with all the vile things he had done, then his head popped up off the floor. He felt the weight of his sins leave him, and his heart was filled with joy and peace that he had never known. Sloan had never danced or sang; he had never done anything that could be even remotely viewed as a celebration. Now he sprang to his feet, began to sing praises to the Lord, and danced his way out of the library. He was a new creation, he knew it, and he could feel it.

Sloan saw the looks of the few people who were there. They gazed upon him as if he had lost his mind. Sloan didn't care what people thought of him; he only cared about his relationship with God and doing God's will.

To that end, as he exited the library, he stopped the first person he came across and asked this question of them.

"Do you know my Lord and Savior, Christ Jesus?"

# ABOUT THE AUTHOR

James H. Henry is first and foremost a follower of Jesus Christ. He lives in Texas with his loving wife, Laura. They have been married for thirty years. James has always loved to read and especially write. He began writing when he was thirteen years old. After a successful career in electrical engineering, James decided it was time to pursue his writing career full-time. To that end, James went back to school. He graduated from Kaplan University with a BS in technical writing. He then graduated from Gonzaga University with a master of arts in communication and leadership.

James taught communication at LeTourneau University as an assistant professor of communication and most recently held the position of technical writer for Johnson and Johnson. James has published a book on public speaking and has written several other books. While James considers these other works important, he considers his latest work (Christian Outlaws) to be a work that God has guided him to and a work that the public needs. It is his hope that you are enlightened and entertained by this work. May God bless you and keep you in His loving arms.

Printed in the USA
CPSIA information can be obtained
at www.ICGtesting.com
CBHW022012030724
11008CB00003B/213